Sinners of Water & Fire

Sinners series book 4

Charity Parkerson

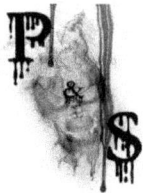

--Warning: This book is intended for mature audiences not offended by explicit representations of sexual activity between consenting adults.

Thank you to every sinner fan. It breaks my heart for this to be the end.

I0682112

3

THE LEGEND OF THE SOCIETY OF SINNERS

Since almost the beginning of time there have been Vampires, but not in the way we have been led to believe. These men were not beasts cursed by the devil, but warriors blessed by God with great strength, agility, and eternal life. A Secret Society formed, where the members used these gifts to defend the innocent against evil. However, as with all things, some were corrupted by such power, and they sought to rule the world.

The Society's Warriors came together in a new fight, one against their own. This new enemy required a new warrior: warriors bred between warriors. These men were to become the men that defeated all evils; new and old. They held a new and powerful gift, a gift that would change the world of Vampires: the power of mind control. These Vampires could bend one's mind to their will and alter one's reality. Each warrior born proved to be unique.

The Mindbenders took their rightful place amongst The Society, causing evil to lose its foothold in the world. It did not take long for the Evil Ones to discover this new power, and they sought to emulate it. However, evil is greedy; expecting quick results. The Evil Ones never considered that true power lies in the giving of life, not in the taking of it.

The Evil Ones chose only the most corrupt of humans for the turning. Their bodies slowly drained of life until the change began, but they were tainted, leaving them as little more than animals. They were an

4

abomination, an insult against nature, and for that, they were forever banished from the sun.

However, what nature meant as a curse became evil's greatest tool. For the night shadowed their scents, and blocked their minds from all others, giving them a safe place to hunt. Their destruction became legendary. It did not take long for the rumors of a new race to reach the ears of The Society, and the Mindbenders were sent to destroy the pack.

Thus, the war between Vampire and Were began. The losses were great for both sides, and the two groups were scattered across the world. As time went on, things changed, and alliances were broken. More and more humans were turned, sometimes by accident, and sometimes with a purpose. Just as not all Vampires were good, it soon became obvious that not all Weres were evil.

As the lines between good and evil became blurred, the fighting lessened. Time and technology also played a role in this, since it became harder to get away with murder, and to deliver vigilante justice. Both sides were forced to change with the times. The Weres moved around, burying their kills, and hiding in the shadows. Recognizing a need for an enforcer, to sort the good from the evil, God sent forth his most trusted and powerful angel, Jazz, to live amongst the Society. Known by most as an Assass`i De`u, or a Killing God, he is feared by all.

As trust in the society faltered, and the world

became more accepting, a few formed separate communities living—sometimes openly—amongst the humans. Nestled high in the mountains of Tennessee, and under the watchful eye of the Assass`i, exists one such community; a town by the name of Jackson Station.

PROLOGUE

"What will I be when I grow up daddy?" my daughter asked as we tucked her into bed.

"You shall be whatever you choose to be," I told her lovingly before thinking to add for good measure, "You shall be a princess, or better yet, you shall be a goddess."

She turned her head to look out her window at the Sea, and her eyes lit up with childlike glee. "Yes. I shall be the Sea Goddess. I will finally get to marry the Star God, and we will never be apart again."

"But you would drown out his light," I told her teasingly, but she shook her head in denial.

"No I won't," she told me firmly. "His star will fall from the heavens. Like all stars must eventually do." Adriana leaned forward with a mischievous glint in her eye as she added to the story. "And now you've been reborn as a real girl, the two of you will live happily ever after." The three of us fell together in a fit of giggles at the ridiculousness of our story. If I had only known, but how could I have known? Oh, how the Gods live to make fools of men!

-Excerpt taken from The New Journal of Alain Moreau

*****

"She's doing it again," Alain called in a stage whisper as he stared out the window above the kitchen sink.

"What?" Adriana asked, and Alain shot her a look of annoyance. "What?" Adriana asked again. "If she's outside, then she can't hear us."

"She's staring at the sky." Alain answered his wife's first question in a normal tone, refusing to admit she was right.

Crossing the room to stand at his side, Adriana peered out the window. "So" she said with a shrug, before reclaiming her seat at the dinner table.

Alain growled. The sound sort of popped out without his permission before he could stop it from happening. Adriana rolled her eyes. "Lots of people gaze at the night sky. It's pretty."

"She's not staring at the night sky," he tried to explain. "She's staring, staring, you know?"

Adriana held his gaze for a moment before her eyes skirted away. He knew she understood what he was saying, but it was difficult, as a parent, to admit you could not help your child. "Our daughter was born as the sun," she said, breaking the silence. Alain turned back to the window as Adriana's words slammed home, slicing through to the heart of the matter. Marissa was a grown woman now and living in her own home. Even though it was right next door, something about her had become unreachable as if she lived a million miles away. Adriana's description of Marissa was simple yet apt.

"Yes," Alain agreed. "She is the sun. She lives surrounded by darkness while the rest of the world basks in the warmth of her glow."

CHAPTER ONE

Their love was legendary...

Once upon a time, the Star God fell in love with the Goddess of the Sea. Their love was a cursed love. His fire would consume her and her water would destroy him. However, at night when the sea reflected the stars, and a person could no longer tell the difference between the two, a new world was created, a world where the two lovers could be together; the dreaming.

Unfortunately, the time came when his star fell from the sky, as all stars eventually do, leaving the Sea Goddess alone.

-Excerpt taken from The Legend of Fire and Water

At the age of sixteen, Lena Simmons quietly passed away in her sleep only to learn it wasn't her time to go. Cast back into the world of the living, she awoke believing it had all been a dream, except she was a little more than she'd been before. From that day on, Lena became obsessed with fortune telling, Tarot cards, dream interpretation, and everything else beyond human understanding. She didn't learn until years later that what she believed to be merely a way to make money was in fact the true gift of second sight—one she now used to benefit the Society.

Flipping over the last card, Lena growled in frustration. Reshuffling the entire deck, she started over, setting up the pyramid once again. She repeated the action twice more before accepting the truth. It was time.

Dan worked quietly at his desk across the room and Lena stared at this profile, unable to work up even an ounce of courage. The sun peeked through the window at his back. The rays danced off his skin, making him glow, and reminding her of the first time she had seen him. It had been at an outdoor wedding. Her best friend's wedding, to be exact. Dan seemed to stand a foot taller than everyone else there. At the first sight of his sweet brown eyes and wide shoulders, Lena had been a goner. He'd been a little harder to convince. Lena smiled at the memory. He hadn't known what hit him when he met her.

"What's so funny?" Dan asked, making her realize she had chuckled aloud. However, his words also yanked her back into the present. A sharp pain stabbed Lena through the heart and she glanced down at the cards laid out in front of her to hide the tears filling her eyes. Blinking them away, she squared her shoulders and stood up to leave.

"I'm going to go see Colin," she said as she swiped a hand over the cards, rearranging them so they couldn't be read. She knew the move was ridiculous, since only her daughter shared her skill, but she couldn't take any chances.

"Is everything okay?" She could hear the concern in Dan's voice, and she almost told him everything, but some things he couldn't fix.

"I saw a reindeer eating oatmeal," she answered, and in a true testament to how familiar Dan was with her nonsensical way of speaking, he merely nodded before going back to his work.

*****

The bungalow where Marissa lived wasn't too far from where her parents were living, but still, it was right on the water's edge. There was a bit of jungle separating them, giving her some seclusion while keeping them close. All that mattered to Marissa was the clear night sky.

"Starlight, star bright," she whispered when she spotted the brightest of the bunch.

"Still repeating that childish lyric, I see." Marissa jumped at the sound of Harold's voice as it carried from the nearby tree line. Pressing a hand to her chest to still the rapid beating, she glanced in his direction. A slight golden glow emanated from his semi-transparent form, making him easy to spot despite the fact she could see the branches behind him through his tall form.

"Damn it, Harold. You scared the shit out of me!" His low masculine chuckle carried on the breeze, making her want to sigh and steadying her heart.

Despite his less than living status, she still couldn't help but notice his blond hair and gorgeous golden-colored eyes. Harold-the-Ghost had shown up one night right after she'd moved into her own home a year ago. She'd thought several times to mention him to her parents, but something always held her back. Perhaps she was ashamed, she mused for the thousandth time. There was no way they would consider seeing a ghost as normal behavior and that was without adding in the fact she found him sexy as hell. With Harold around, she felt complete, yet at the same time, she realized how ridiculous she would sound saying those words aloud to anyone else. At times, she experienced a disconnection with reality that left her wondering how long she might cling to this world. To distract herself from the depressing thought, she went back to watching the sky. "Most people think it's merely a nursery rhyme," she admitted. "But in truth, it's a spell," Marissa explained.

"What does this spell do exactly?" Harold asked, sounding curious instead of disbelieving as she'd been expecting.

"It captures the attention of one star—if you manage to actually spot the brightest star in the sky, that is. In theory, this spell will hold that star's attention long enough for you to request one favor from it."

"Thus explaining the mythology behind wishing on a star," he said, proving he understood her.

13

"Exactly," she agreed brightly, meeting his eyes once more. With his arms crossed over his broad chest and leaning against the tree, he seemed ready to keep her company for the rest of the night.

"So what favor are you requesting?"

"I can't tell you that or it won't come true," she answered, exasperated.

"Ah, so that part of the nursery rhyme is true, then?"

"Well, yeah, a star has its pride, you know? Especially the brightest one. He can't let the other stars know he's been captured by a mere druid priestess."

Harold laughed at what he must've thought was silly reasoning. However, he of all people understood she believed in things most people didn't. After all, she believed in him, and here he was.

"Perhaps the star is only pretending to be ensnared by your spell," he said, attempting to hide his mirth.

"What would be the point in that?"

"As you said, a star has its pride," he answered as he devoured her body with his eyes. "So it uses your spell as an excuse to grant your every desire."

Marissa's skin tingled with awareness, which he brought to life by his words and hot look. Gritting the back of her teeth against the desire to reach out for him, and knowing he was not really there, she changed the subject.

"What brings you around tonight?"

"I missed you," he answered, causing her heart to soar for a moment before, once again, reality set in. She looked down at her feet in an attempt to hide her reaction. "I shouldn't have said that," he began, and she cut him off.

"I dreamed about you last night." Heat flooded her face at the confession. She knew it must be the shade of a strawberry, but she lifted her eyes to his, holding his stare steadily, as if daring him to mock her words. For a moment, she could've sworn a look of triumph passed over his face, but it was gone as quickly as it appeared.

"What was the dream about?"

Marissa had thought it was impossible to be any more embarrassed than she already was. At his question, she discovered a whole new level of humiliation.

"Um," she stuttered before admitting, "I don't want to tell you."

"Oh," he crowed. "It was that kind of dream, was it?" While his eyes were shining with mirth, her face was on fire, and she really wanted kick him.

"Shut up," she hissed.

"Ever as you command," he said, but she could still hear the laughter in his voice.

Fanning her face, Marissa practically danced in place in her discomfort.

"Are you having some sort of fit?" Adriana, Marissa's mom, asked, slicing through her mortification.

Marissa hadn't heard her approach. She shot a nervous glimpse at the tree line to find Harold gone.

"I was attempting a spell." Marissa answered Adriana's question absently while searching for any sign Harold was still hanging around. When her mom remained silent, Marissa glanced over to find her watching her closely. She pasted a fake smile on her face to ease her mother's obvious concern.

"Okay," Adriana said, drawing out the word and sounding as if she didn't believe her, which was a spot-on observation, since Marissa was lying.

"I came out here to let you know I got a call from Colin. He's going to be here tomorrow." Concerns over Harold's whereabouts were temporarily forgotten in the excitement over the prospect of seeing Colin–the-Tracker. Although Colin was thousands of years old, he acted and appeared closer to the age of twenty. Marissa had always been genuinely fond of him. However, his position as a tracker for the Society meant he couldn't come around as often as she'd like.

"How long is he going to stay?"

"Probably not that long," Adriana admitted. "But if I know him, he'll try to spend as much time as he can with us."

A hint of worry wormed its way into Marissa's excitement at the odd undertone in Adriana's voice. "Is he here on Society business?"

A tracker was the equivalent of the police for the Society and since Colin's "special gift" was the ability to transform his appearance, he was perfectly suited for the job of tracking down rogue Vampires. The Society comprised purebred Vampires. Occasionally, after years of living, one would become bored with eternal life and do crazy things such as killing humans or turning them into taint-blooded monsters. That's where the trackers came in.

"I'm sure he probably has some form of business to attend to in the area and we are an added bonus along the way." Although Adriana smiled as she said the words, she twisted her hands nervously, giving away her thoughts. They hadn't dealt with any trouble in the area since before Marissa was born. The thought of a rogue in the area was, at the very least, disheartening.

"Well, we'll enjoy his company while he's here," Marissa chirped, hoping her over-the-top enthusiasm would calm her mother's fears.

It wasn't until Marissa was pulling back the sheets of her bed that her worry fell away and her thoughts returned to Harold. Had he disappeared because he wanted no one to know about him? With a heavy heart, Marissa climbed in bed and clutched her pillow to her chest. He'd said he missed her. Smiling at the memory of those words, she turned on her side. As sleep overtook her, she heard his voice whispering in her ear. His fingers skimmed over her hip, causing her nipples to harden. "Let's talk about that dream."

CHAPTER TWO

"The limo ride to the hotel was a luxurious one, but once inside the room, when he pulled back the cover on the tiny bed, the sheets were covered with a light smattering of dirt and grime, making them appear more brown than white. I didn't care because we were together. I smiled as I took a running leap onto the bed. He threw himself down beside me. Our laughter echoed off the walls as we bounced. My father, of all people, told me to write down every detail. He says it is not the dream that holds the most importance. Instead, it's the tiny moments and feelings involved in the nighttime illusion. What I remember the most was the color of his eyes. They were blue, not any blue, but the sort of blue you find on a flower on an unexplored hill. They were so close to my own. He was mere inches from me, and the overwhelming feeling of love I felt in that moment caused my lungs to cease working. Funny how I don't remember taking a single breath or even missing oxygen in that moment. I suppose air isn't important in Dreamland. My life was the same as it is every day, yet nothing else existed for me but him. I didn't have a single thought. The only thing real in that fantasy world was my love for that man. Things weren't meant to be this way. He felt it too. I could see it, sense it, and taste it. He smiled, and it reached even his eyes as he leaned in to kiss me. The love in his eyes and the phantom weight of his body pressed against mine, those are the things that lingered when my eyes opened, allowing the

last wisps of the dream to fade away. That and the blue of his eyes are the things I cannot shake from my mind, so what do I take away from this dream? If dreams predict the future, if you can read the signs and determine what cannot be seen through mortal eyes, then which detail was the most important? Was it the dirty bed, the color of his eyes, or the love that was choking me? Perhaps, it was all three, but do you know what I think? I think I wasn't alone in that dream. I think wherever he is, he felt it too. Our love brought us together again if only in the dreaming."

-Taken from the Dream Journal of Marissa Moreau

Heru had taken the name Harold before his death and for that reason, he introduced himself to Marissa using that name. He'd returned to the land of the gods, and was once again Heru, except with some major changes. He was the fallen star now and could no longer shine in the night sky or create a dreamland for others by simply casting a glow upon the sea. However, he could still visit that magical place to see Marissa. Oh, how the fates must have laughed when he died in the mortal realm, knowing Marissa was a druid priestess now. If she ever died, her soul would not visit this place. Instead, she would continue to be reborn for eternity. His bargain with the devil was complete.

The fact he could breach the mortal realm in spirit form was one part pleasure and two parts torment … especially today as he watched another man's attempt to win Marissa's heart. If only she would remember that she was his Goddess, then no other man would stand a chance, of that he was certain.

Heru was never one to care for the looks of another man. Today, he cataloged every asset of his opponent. Colin-the-Tracker's green eyes and blond hair might not have been a threat to Heru if those were the only weapons the ancient Vampire held in his arsenal. However, he also possessed an intelligent mind that presented itself as witty remarks to Marissa's every statement. He was a dangerous combination. The beast inside Heru wanted to rip Colin's head off every time he caused Marissa to laugh. Her laughter belonged to him. He'd be damned if he allowed Colin to steal it from him.

Marissa covered her mouth with both hands, holding back another giggle. Heru resisted the urge to show himself to the room. Since the last thing he wanted was for Marissa to suspect him of watching her all day, he focused his attentions on Marissa instead of Colin, hoping to stem his growing jealousy.

Marissa thought she caught sight of Harold once, but he disappeared as quickly as he appeared. She knew he was there, despite not being able to see him. She could feel his presence with every molecule of her being. When he was around, her senses fired to life and gravitated toward him.

"What brings you to town?" she asked Colin, in an

attempt to focus on reality.

"Perhaps I came for you," he suggested, and Marissa blinked in confusion. Colin had never openly flirted with her before, but his tone left little doubt he was now. She'd never pictured him in that light. However, his eyes were very sparkly, and his body was enough to make any girl feel all gooey inside.

Eyeing his muscled jawline, she watched in fascination as a seductive smile touched his lips, causing her to blush. She wasn't interested in Colin in that way, but sometimes she worried she'd simply disconnect to the point she ceased to exist.

"Did you come for me?" she asked, sounding more seductive than she intended.

"Not yet," he answered boldly, but his eyes drifted toward the doorway as her father entered the room. Standing, Colin crossed the room to greet Alain. Both men were equal in height but clashed in coloration. Whereas Colin was an angelic blond, her father appeared every inch the dark Celtic of old he was. Together, they looked like a glowing example of an angel meeting the devil.

A slight breeze brushed across her neck, lifting her hair, and causing chill bumps to form on her skin. Invisible lips touched her neck. She heard Harold's whispered voice inside her head. "You're mine."

With a gasp, Marissa's teacup slipped from her fingers, hitting the floor, and making a tiny clink sound as it landed on the carpet. The men turned in her direction. She quickly bent, snatching it back up. "Sorry. Mom would die if I broke one of these," she said, waving the tiny cup in an attempt to explain away her reaction.

Marissa listened with half an ear as Colin filled her father in on the details of his assignment. She gathered from their discussion that a tainted man by the name of Rani had been spotted nearby. Colin had been sent in to investigate. In truth, for the most part, all Marissa was gleaning from the conversation was blah blah blah, while her mind remained completely focused on Harold.

"In the meantime, I intend to distract Marissa with my charms," Colin said, pulling her from her thoughts and back into the present.

"Good. She could use a distraction," Alain said, showing no shame over selling out his own daughter. Marissa tittered nervously and admonished her father, but he cut her off at the pass.

"I'll leave you two alone. I have a wife I could entertain," he said, wiggling his eyebrows and making Marissa groan in mortification.

Colin turned his smiling eyes in her direction as soon as they were alone.

"Hmm, seems I have you all to myself now. With your father's approval, at that."

As soon as the words left Colin's mouth, Marissa felt the weight of Harold's hand on her upper thigh. She had to work at keeping a moan from falling from her lips as his touch moved upward. "He has nothing," Harold said, his voice running through her head. She knew when Colin didn't react, she was the only one who could hear him.

Testing a theory, Marissa kicked her smile up a notch. "What do you intend to do with me?" she asked, her question meant for both men.

"As much as you'll allow," Colin answered at the same time as Harold said, "You'll pay for this, minx."

Her inner thigh tingled as he ran his fingers up it. The slight pressure between her legs warned her Harold had reached his goal. Seizing a nearby throw pillow, Marissa covered her lap. It was half in fear of Colin noticing anything strange. She also needed to have some barrier between them, should Colin attempt to move on her offer.

Colin still gave no hint he sensed anything out of the ordinary, nor did he do anything more than flirt with her. Taking advantage of the situation, Marissa kept up a steady banter with Colin, enticing Harold to become bolder with each passing moment. With each bat of her eyes and flip of hair, there was bold stroke of her clit.

Before long, Marissa was batting her eyes and flipping her hair so often she imagined it looked like she was having a seizure.

With her body on fire and on the edge of coming right then, she was reminded of an old movie she'd once seen. The main character loudly faked an orgasm in a restaurant as everyone around her watched. The only problem was Marissa was near to having the real experience and that would be a hard one to explain. She felt certain the leather couch beneath her would have permanent indentations from her fingernails.

She was barely restraining herself as it was and she knew it was time to end the game before Colin busted her or she screamed "Yes, yes" at the top of her lungs.

Jumping to her feet and causing the pillow to fall to the floor, Marissa smiled gleamingly at Colin. "It's been great chatting with you, but I've just remembered I forgot . . ." She scrambled for an excuse, but a red haze of lust slowed down her thought process. ". . . something," she finally tacked on lamely.

Thankfully, instead of looking suspicious, as she feared, he appeared smug, as if he thought his flirtations had addled her brain. Out of respect, Colin stood as well. As she made her hasty retreat, he called at her back, "I'll drop by again tomorrow."

Marissa threw a tiny wave over her shoulder to let him know she heard, but she didn't slow her steps.

"Marissa," Colin called, freezing her in her tracks right before she made it to the door. "If I'm still around tomorrow, will you go out with me?"

There was something odd in his tone. It caused her to turn around. She looked at him closer as her mind scrambled for an answer.

"Do you not plan on being around?" she asked in an attempt at buying some time.

An indecipherable look flashed across his face before returning to his earlier flirtatious smile. "Of course," he answered smoothly.

"Then I'll answer you tomorrow," she told him, using her most cheeky tone before making a run for it. She didn't stop again until her back was pressed against the inside her closed front door.

The house felt empty. She knew Harold was gone. Her face burned with mortification at the thought of what she'd done. She groaned aloud as the picture of her flipping her hair over her shoulder flashed across her mind. Covering her face with both hands, she let a tiny bubble of hysterical laughter escape. If it turned out Harold only existed in her mind, she would have to move to the mountains and become a hermit so she could be crazy in private.

*****

The five stages of grief were more like two for Colin: anger and acceptance. He refused to feel the two emotions separately. Compared to a few of the other immortals, he was considered an ancient as he'd seen thousands of years pass. Life as a tracker was exhausting. However, no matter how tired he might be, he still wasn't ready to die. Although his death was inevitable, planned out way before his birth, that didn't mean he had to be happy about it.

Sealing the plain white envelope, Colin tilted the lamp to the side and tucked the letter underneath the edge. He didn't bother addressing it, as Jazz would make sure it ended up in the right hands. With his final task complete, Colin bowed his head and sucked in a fortifying breath. Without turning, he knew the demon had arrived by the sick feeling of dread churning in his gut. The stench of rotting flesh hung heavy in the air.

"Do you pray for your soul?" asked a hissing voice from behind him.

Letting out a mirthless laugh, Colin slipped his hand inside his jacket, wrapping his fingers around a heavy silver dagger.

"Do you fear for yours?" he asked, taunting death.

*****

Curled on her side, Marissa could feel the first wisps of sleep closing in when warmth surrounded her, almost as if someone was hugging her. Her eyes shot open.

"Close your eyes," Harold whispered against her ear.

The silkiness of his voice left her hypnotized as if he was drugging her mind. "None of this is real," he reminded her. At his words, her lids lifted again, and she protested.

"But I want it to be real. I want to be with you." She could hear the desperation in her voice, but she no longer cared. She'd waited all day for him to reappear, and now that he was finally here, she needed him to know she wanted him here with her.

"Shhh," he soothed. "This place isn't real, but we are."

The force of his convictions finally gave her the push she needed to let go of the real world. "Yes," she agreed as her eyes slid closed. As soon as she could no longer see the room, it fell away completely. His body became a tangible weight against hers. His lips touched the side of her neck as his hand found the hem of her nightgown. The material rose over her hip, bunching around her waist as his palm slid over her skin, until his hand came to rest between her breasts. Keeping her eyes squeezed tightly closed, she silently prayed he wouldn't disappear. Her body, still humming from his touch earlier in the day, fired back to life. A moan escaped from her throat. Her feet moved restlessly against the sheets.

"It's all a dream," he said quietly, attempting to hypnotize her mind. When the room plunged into darkness for a moment before hundreds of candles flared to life around them, Heru knew she'd crossed over into the dreaming. A surge of triumph shot through his chest as he nudged Marissa onto her back. Leaning on one elbow, he stared down at her, soaking in every detail of her face. Had her parents never wondered over the differences between her and themselves? Both of her parents were dark-haired with some variation of green to their eyes, while Marissa's hair was blonde to the point of almost being white, and her eyes were the clearest blue. She possessed all the features and coloration of a Goddess. It couldn't be more obvious. Her eyes fluttered open, and she smiled at the sight of him. He loved that sweet smile. Of course, he loved everything about her.

"Did you know your eyes are a different color in my dreams?" she asked, taking him by surprise. He searched for every possible pitfall before answering.

"I've lived more than one life," he admitted, deciding to go with a hint of the truth. She nodded her understanding. As a druid, no one could appreciate the concept more than she could. Without giving her time to think over his answer, he leaned in and touched his lips to hers. If he still had a heart to beat, he knew that it would've been racing out of chest as their tongues brushed. The taste of her was as familiar to him as his reflection. He burned to know if the rest of her still tasted the same. Moving from her mouth to her throat, he sucked lightly at the skin at her pulse before traveling on to her collarbone. Gripping her wrists with one hand, he held her hands trapped above her head as he used his free hand to lift her gown until her breasts were bare. Dipping his head, he sucked the tip of one hardened nipple into his mouth, flattening his tongue against it. Marissa writhed beneath his touch and fought against his hold until he released her hands. Her fingernails bit into his shoulders as he scooted further down the bed. Pausing at her navel, he placed a fleeting kiss above it before circling it with his tongue.

"Please," she begged. "No more teasing."

"Ever as you command," he said quietly against her skin. He reached between their bodies and stroked her wet folds. His dick was throbbing and begging to be touched, but he ignored it as he lowered his head between her legs. The smooth skin of her inner thigh brushed against his cheek as she hooked her knee over his shoulder. Lifting her hips, she pressed closer to his mouth as he delved inside her canal with his fingers. His cock twitched and a drop of moisture escaped its head as she squeezed her muscles around them. He slowly traced the lines that were hiding her love button from him with his tongue, determined to draw out her pleasure. She pulled his hair in retaliation, and he pushed her knees wide, holding her open for his ministrations. Devouring her, he nipped at her clit before licking it in apology. She moaned and his balls drew up tight at the sound. His body recognized its master. He pumped two fingers inside her while circling her clit with his tongue. He pictured his dick buried inside the warm wet heat surrounding his fingers and nearly lost control. When he felt her tense beneath him, he increased his speed and pressure until he felt her body jerk as she cried out in release. Her ragged breathing sounded loud in the otherwise silent room and he ran his lips across her thigh. His inner turmoil after touching her was almost frightening in its intensity and he feared what he might do. Her fingers fluttered across his shoulder and he closed his eyes to savor her touch. He wanted to memorize every sensation to keep him warm when they were apart.

"I miss you so much when you're not here, Heru," Marissa said, causing his heart to break. He wondered for the thousandth time if he should leave her alone and allow her to have a normal life instead of this half-life she lived with him.

"Marissa, I," he began, before he realized that she had used his real name. However, before he could say what was rushing to his lips, he found himself once again blinking against the bright light of the heavens. With his mental energy depleted, his time, once again, was up. In a fit of rage, Heru snatched up the nearest chair, tossing it against the wall. Splinters flew in every direction, but it did little to calm him. Scrubbing at his scalp in frustration, he quietly begged for an answer. He wanted to be with Marissa. He craved her every breath, yet life continuously denied him at every turn. Next time, he vowed, she would hear what he had been robbed of saying to her tonight. Geb appeared at his side, placing a loving hand on his shoulder and giving it a light squeeze. Even though Heru knew his father meant to be comforting, he still found that he could not look him in the eye.

"Why?" Heru asked, hearing the desperation in his voice but unable to mask it. "When I came to you on bended knee, and begged for your help, you swore that you didn't have the power to take her from the Sea."

"I said that I couldn't steal away with a Goddess," Geb clarified. "However, I didn't say I couldn't coax her into joining you in the mortal realm."

His father's words shocked Heru into meeting his gaze. "Thank you," he said, never meaning anything more than he did in that moment. "Even though it didn't work out where we could be together, I appreciate that you tried."

"There is nothing I wouldn't do for you," Geb said, astounding him with the blazing intensity of his voice.

CHAPTER THREE

It is the nature of life to want what is just out of our reach, long for more than we should, and lust for things we dare not confess. The Goddess of the Sea accepted that truth with heavy heart when a soldier of the sky caught her attention. He was no boy with cherub cheeks and laughing eyes. He was a man of solid muscle, calculating eyes, and wicked smiles. She wanted to accept that he was something she would never have, and in truth, she tried. That was until he looked her way. Nature lost a great battle that night, one that would go down in history, and the tale would pass from generation to generation.

"Starlight. Star bright. I see a star I would like. Send him down now as I command so he may grant my every demand. I swear that I will not harm his fire as he fulfills my every desire," Goddess Marissa whispered as she stared intently at the brightest star in the sky.

In a flash of light, he appeared, hovering mere inches above the water. Flipped on his head with his feet floating above him, he kept his hands clasped behind his back. Tiny flames flickered from every inch of his golden body, making him look like a fiery raindrop clinging from a cloud.

"Ever as you command," the Golden God answered, opening endless possibilities for Marissa.

-Excerpt taken from The Legend of Fire and Water

Letting herself in her parent's back door, Marissa went in search of her mom, feeling more bogged down than she had in years. A night with a blinding orgasm followed by zero sleep while crying her eyes out could do that for a woman. She had seen her worst dreams come true. She had finally spoken Heru's real name, and he had disappeared. What if years of longing had finally caused her mind to snap and Heru existed nowhere but in her mind? The thought caused her to miss a step as the feeling of being punched in the gut overtook her once more. Catching sight of Adriana standing at the sink washing dishes, Marissa moved to stand at her side. Grabbing a nearby towel, she silently helped. She needed something to keep her busy.

"Your father has gone to pick up Colin, and I was straightening up," she explained. Marissa nodded that she'd heard, but her thoughts remained with Heru and wherever he'd gone.

"It was good to see you connecting with Colin yesterday," Adriana said, pulling Marissa from her worries and making her curious over the cautious note in her voice.

"You say that as if you think I'll become some old spinster." Marissa was only half joking. When Adriana remained silent a moment too long, she realized her mother feared exactly that.

"Come on, Mom. I don't need a man to make me

happy. I'm perfectly content on my own."

"I know," Adriana cried, surprising her. "That's the problem. You seem to withdraw a little more every day and you're living on your own now." She waved her arms as if searching for the right words and sending bubbles flying. "And I'm your mother. It's my right to worry."

Marissa hated knowing she caused her mother concern, and she wanted to soothe her fears. However, she also felt the need to be as honest as she could without revealing too much.

"I'm happier when I'm alone." When Adriana looked crestfallen, Marissa bumped her with her hip.

"Don't look like that," she chided. "There's nothing wrong with me. It's only the silence suits me better."

As Adriana grumbled something about how she had always been a reflective child, Marissa secretly hoped that she had not been lying. There wasn't anything wrong with her, right?

The sound of the back door opening yanked Marissa from that depressing thought, and she turned to find Alain wearing a grim expression. She knew immediately something was wrong. "What's happened?" Adriana asked, stealing Marissa's question.

"Colin is dead," he answered. His solemn tone

loaned truth to his words as Marissa wanted to call them a lie.

A roar of denial exploded inside her head as the announcement seemed to suck all sound from the universe, and Marissa could not even hear the pounding of her own heart racing in her chest any longer. Absently, she recognized that she was about to faint, but it wasn't enough to stop the world from going black before her eyes.

*****

He pointed out over the water. "Do you see how many places the stars touch the water?" When she nodded, he confessed, "They search for you. I have every single one of them searching for you."

"Why?" she asked, astounded by his admission.

"Because I love you and I don't want to lose you," he answered, stealing away her breath.

*****

Although shaken, Marissa stayed conscious as her mother explained that Alain had only found ashes when he had gone to fetch Colin. It was unbelievable to her she'd been flirting with him in this very house a day earlier and now she would never see his smiling face again. He'd known he would die. That one thought continued to plague her as she listened to her mom speaking. She couldn't explain how she knew, but she was positive that's what she'd seen flash across his face right before leaving. She wasn't surprised when her father disappeared and then reappeared a few minutes later with Jazz in tow. Jazz Anderson was an Assass`i De`u, an angel who was one of God's greatest warriors in Heaven sent to live on Earth as protection for humans and enforcer for God himself. He was believed to be the only one currently in existence. It was also rumored that he had a direct line to the heavens and could freely travel between the realms. His name alone was enough to strike fear into the hearts of immortals, but his appearance left no doubt that every whispered story that Marissa had heard about him was true. His six-foot-six frame towered over every other person in the room and his unnaturally violet-colored eyes shined in a way that could not be mistaken for human eyes. The dark hue of his skin hinted at an Asian descent, but the tattoo that ran the length of one side of his body was the true marking of his rank, and showed where the hand of God had touched him. His presence alone left Marissa feeling comforted, and she knew Colin would get the justice he deserved.

"We need Heru," Jazz announced, skipping all niceties, and a chill raced over Marissa's skin at the name.

"Who is Heru?" Adriana asked at the same time as Alain said, "I thought he was dead."

Jazz shook his head as he chose a seat at the kitchen table directly across from Marissa. "Yes and no. While it is true his mortal body passed from this life, it is more like he's trapped in the Hall of the Gods."

Marissa sat in a silent shock while Adriana seemed shaken to the point where she no longer cared about etiquette.

"Who is Heru?" she repeated. "What can he do to help, and how is he supposed to help us if he's stuck in the Hall the Gods?"

Every eye turned in Adriana's direction at her line of questioning.

"Don't look at me as if I have two heads," she snapped. Marissa understood her pain. Colin had saved her mother's life once, and she expected Jazz to announce the imminent death of the man responsible.

Thankfully, instead of chastising Adriana for her rudeness, Jazz patiently answered her questions. "Heru is the son of Geb, but most people know him as the Star God. However, after his fall to Earth, he struck a deal with the demon God, Ranihura, to forget who he was. In exchange for easing his pain, he appointed Heru the task of acquiring the Kamilah. The problem is that once Heru forgot his past, the demon kept him as a slave for many years."

At Jazz's answer, Marissa gasped so hard that she

nearly choked and fell into a coughing fit. Tears stung the backs of her eyes as she gasped for air. Adriana placed a hand on Marissa's knee, and Marissa gave her hand a pat to let her know she was okay even though she wasn't. Marissa thought she would to be sick.

"The Star God is real?" Adriana said, sounding as if she was choking. "And you wish to bring him here?"

A tiny sob escaped Marissa's lips as her shock faded. This whole time Jazz had the power to bring them together. Mistaking the reason behind her heartache, Adriana gave Marissa's knee another pat.

"I'm sorry," Adriana said in apology. "But we're already dealing with one murderer in this town and he's talking about bring a God here that's been enslaved by a demon. I can't see how that will help anything."

Marissa kept expecting Jazz to lash out at her mother, but his expression never changed as he offered an explanation.

"Yes, the Star God is real, but he will harm no one. I also do not intend to bring him back to this town, but rather to Jackson Station where we have more reinforcements in place. I believe the taint named Rani, who Colin was hunting, is in truth the demon Ranihura, and only Heru has the power to stop him."

"How do you intend to steal him from the heavens?" Alain asked, giving voice to the biggest obstacle they faced.

"I will travel to the Hall of the Gods and carry him out if necessary. It will not be easy," he said, answering Alain's question, but holding Marissa's gaze as if attempting to prepare her for the upcoming challenge. "In the meantime," he continued, transferring his attention back to Alain. "I ask that the three of you travel to Jackson Station where we can better protect you. In addition, it will lure Rani away from this place, keeping the innocent people of this town safe."

Alain waved off Jazz's concern. "We are more than capable of taking care of our own and besides, he has no reason to follow us or target our family. Demons have little use for druids. We cannot trade our souls."

Jazz took on an indecipherable look.

"What are not telling us?" Adriana asked carefully.

Jazz remained silent for so long that Marissa hoped that he would not answer, and when he did, his words came out haltingly as if he didn't want to part with the information. "Before Heru's death, he defied Rani by keeping the Kamilah safe instead of capturing her as ordered." Marissa only knew what the Kamilah was because she had heard her story told many times. Kamilah was not an object, but instead a beautiful woman who went by the name Kim. Kim could control dreams and plant ideas into the minds of the entire world. For that reason, many considered her the most powerful weapon in existence, and would do anything to possess her. Marissa wasn't surprised that a demon would want to take control of her.

"Do you think he seeks to use us to learn the location of the Kamilah?" Alain asked.

Jazz shook his head. "No, he would know by now she is too powerful for him to control, but he did not take Heru's broken bargain lightly, and he will come here to seek his revenge on Heru by destroying the one thing he held most dear: the Sea Goddess."

Marissa felt her heart drop at his words. There was no avoiding it now.

"I still don't understand what that has to do with us."

At Adriana's words, Jazz turned his violet gaze in Marissa's direction and held her stare steadily until she turned her face away from his silent accusations.

"It has everything to do with your family," he answered slowly. "Marissa is the Sea Goddess."

Silence filled the room and Marissa could feel the eyes upon her, but she kept her gaze locked on the corner. She'd tried so many times as a child to tell them everything, but they smiled and praised her imagination until she gave up. Feeling the warmth against her side, she moved closer to it, and Jazz stared over her shoulder.

"Save your energy and prepare for battle," Jazz commanded, but the warmth remained in place.

"What's going on?" Adriana asked. Confusion and tears heavily laced her voice.

Wind whipped through the room and the power of her father's temper could be felt as if it were a tangible thing. She met his eyes hoping to make him understand, but they glowed bright, stealing away that expectation. Raising his hand, he slammed his palm down upon the table, sending a wave of pure energy rippling throughout the room. Sparks of magic bounced off the walls until Heru's semi-transparent form appeared for all to see. Adriana's gasp was loud enough to be heard, but Heru kept his eyes locked on Marissa. Kneeling beside her chair, Heru grasped her hands in his.

"If we lose this fight, they will seal my gate to you."

Marissa's eyes fell closed at Heru's warning and tears fought to fall. Her nose burned and throat swelled, leaving her unable to speak. Letting go of his hand, she made a helpless gesture, and another sob broke loose.

"Don't cry," he soothed. "I will find my way back to you. I swear it."

Leaning forward, she touched her forehead to his and his form solidified for a moment.

"If they seal the gate, I will storm the heavens," she

vowed. Opening her eyes, she held his gaze so he could see the honesty behind her words. "I love you. I gave up one life for you and I will give a thousand more." She quickly pressed her lips to his. "Go, stay safe, and come home to me."

"Ever as you command," he said as he disappeared. As soon as Heru was gone, Adriana wrapped her arms around Marissa from behind and she collapsed against her. The tears ran unchecked down Marissa's face as she stared at the place where Heru had been while accepting the comfort only a mother could give.

CHAPTER FOUR

Goddess Marissa cast her spell upon the sky each night, and Heru always appeared before the final word left her lips. However, instead of naming her wish, she would keep him there until right before dawn with a promise to release him from his service to her the next night.

"Marissa, you promised," he reminded her as it became obvious that night would be no different.

"What is that mark on your arm?" she asked, changing the subject.

He glanced over at the black star with a red lightning bolt streaking through it that covered her upper bicep. "It is the mark of a warrior," he answered with a shrug. "Now stop avoiding it. You promised," he repeated.

"I'm embarrassed," she admitted with a blush.

He felt a smile tug at the corners of his mouth at her confession. "If you'd like, you may whisper it in my ear. No one else shall ever know the words you speak."

Looking unsure for a moment, she finally nodded in agreement. A surge of triumph ran through his veins as he dropped closer to the sea. Stretching upward, her lips brushed his ear. But as she opened her mouth to speak, he turned his head, and captured her lips with his own.

Fire raced through Heru that had nothing to do with his flame and light exploded around them. The real world fell away, and he was holding Marissa in his arms as he never thought he would. Happiness overrode his shock as he stared down into her eyes.

"I burn hotter for you than any star in the sky," he confessed.

"My love is deeper than the sea," she whispered back.

-Excerpt from the Legend of Fire and Water

Jackson Station made the hair on her arms stand up; that was the best way Marissa could describe how the town interacted with her magic. The small community was one of the few places in the world where all different types of supernatural creatures lived openly among humans. If you were born here, you didn't leave here, and if you came here, it was for a reason. Jazz had insisted that she leave right away while her parents stayed behind to cast magical wards around their homes. Although Marissa could travel any place in the world in the blink of an eye, a handy spell she'd learned at a young age, she didn't leave Martinique often. Being away from the Sea always made her feel as if a thousand tiny ants covered her skin, and as its Goddess, she was not as powerful away from its life-giving energy. To keep from tearing her own hair out, Marissa concentrated on her surroundings.

Her Aunt Lena wasn't really her aunt, but sense of family is a bit strange for a person who lives forever. Lena had jumped way over the line of eccentricity long ago, but positive vibes flowed from her body, drawing Marissa to her side. It was soothing to Marissa's overwrought nerves. Lena's bright pink hair and flowing green dress stood out like a beacon in the overcrowded room, which was saying something, since her daughter Kera had glowing blue hair. Despite Kera's wild appearance, she was the more levelheaded of the two. Although the pair were human, they were both clairvoyant, and therefore powerful in their own right. Kera's husband, Weave, did not match his name in any way. He could have been the poster boy for Army recruits or posed for the cover of GQ. His dark hair was cut military short and working as a professional fighter left every inch of his body hardened with muscle. Despite his clean-cut exterior, there was something dark about him. It was as if he'd seen a glimpse of Hell and could not erase the memory of it. It was on the tip of Marissa's tongue to ask him his story, but she suppressed the urge out of propriety.

Everyone seemed to be holding their breath as they waited for Jazz's metaphysical return. When first told of Jazz's plan, she'd conjured a picture of a staircase to Heaven appearing at his feet, and she would simply wait for that staircase to reappear for his return. She realized now how ridiculous that notion had been. Of all people, she should have been more aware of the fact that the mind is the fastest way to travel and the place we are all most powerful. Of course, that fact left them all staring at a meditating Jazz, and wondering if he would find his way in.

Marissa attempted to hold a conversation with Lena, but she jumped at every sound, and Lena seemed even more distracted than usual.

Jazz's wife, Cherish, who had been pacing a circle around Jazz's body, finally came to sit between Lena and Marissa on the couch.

"How long does it take to travel between realms?" Marissa asked, curious as to how much longer she would have to suffer. Cherish brought her hand to her mouth and chewed on her cuticles nervously.

"I don't know," she answered around her thumb. "As far as I know, Jazz has not done this since we've been together."

Cherish was easily the most strikingly gorgeous woman that Marissa had ever seen. Her jet-black hair and ink-colored eyes, coupled with her perfect pale skin, caused her to stand out in a crowd. However, today her hair was piled on top of her head and her shirt wrinkled up in several places. Her unkempt appearance gave away her nervousness. Lena leaned closer to Cherish and gave her a comforting pat on the back.

"Don't worry, sweetie. It's not as if they'll keep him

or anything," Lena reassured.

Cherish sucked in a horrified breath at Lena's words. "Oh my God. Do you think that's a possibility?" she asked. "I mean, once he gets there, they could decide not to let him come home, right?" Without waiting for an answer, she chanted, "Shit. Shit. Shit," before jumping back to her feet and pacing the room once more. Lena glanced at Marissa and pulled a face.

"Oops," she whispered, making Marissa smile despite the situation. Her light mood didn't last long as Lena returned to her own worries and Marissa went back to wanting to crawl out her own skin. The tiny wooden cabin where Jazz and Cherish lived, while the perfect size for the couple, seemed miniscule with so many people stuffed into its living room. A huge stone fireplace took up most of the room and there was only a couch and recliner for seating. Weave carried the chairs from the kitchen table into the room so that everyone would have a place to sit, but they had not needed them yet, since Cherish continued to pace and Dan stood with his back to the room as he stared out the window. Her parents had not yet arrived since they'd traveled to Jackson Station by mortal means hoping Rani would follow them and buy the town extra time to plan.

Jazz slumped forward on a gasp and a slash of blood appeared across his back, taking them all by surprise. Cherish let out a cry in horror, but they all remained frozen in place. With her hand pressed to her chest,

Marissa bent over for a second and sucked in a breath, before righting herself once more. The battle had begun.

*****

The sound of the dense oak door slamming against the stone palace wall echoed loudly throughout the room. Of course, it only took the tiniest noise to cause a soul's ears to ring in the heavens. It was a vast, empty, and golden chasm of nothingness. It could either be viewed as peaceful or drive a man insane, depending upon the blackness of his own soul. Jazz froze in place, but when no one came running at the loud noise, he crept further inside. The room, along with everything inside it, was solid white. Two of the walls were covered from floor to ceiling in mirrors that reflected the bleached room back at itself. Two steps in, Jazz knew something was wrong. The hair stood on the back of his neck and the sensation that someone was watching his every move crawled over his skin. Casting his gaze around the room, the mirrors caught his eye as he realized what was missing in their reflection: him. Twisting his wrist, he allowed the silver sword hidden within his sleeve to slip down into his hand as he readied himself for what lurked out of sight. The Sig Sauer pressing into the small of his back brought him a level of comfort even though he had his doubts about the gun's ability to harm anything this side of the realm. The door slammed closed behind him and the room transformed. The mirrors disappeared, exposing them as an illusion, and revealed the creatures hidden within the depths of the room.

Massive black wings sprouted from their shoulders, causing the seven-foot humanlike beings to appear closer to nine feet in height. They were each different in coloration, but shared the same warrior-like build. With weapons strapped across their bare chests and kilts that hung to their knees, they looked like a Scottish clan of fallen angels. Jazz knew without looking they had him surrounded. Bracing his feet apart, he readied for battle. Expecting a head-on fight, Jazz was caught off guard by the blade slicing across his back. The blow knocked him to his knees, but he quickly jumped back to his feet, ignoring the burning sensation. When the one responsible moved in for a second blow, Jazz kicked out, swiping the legs out from beneath him, and bringing him down. Without giving him a chance to recover, Jazz drew back his sword, intent on taking his life in exchange for the blood that still trickled down the back of Jazz's jacket.

"Enough!" cried one creature, and Jazz met his gaze with his sword still lifted over his head. The creature's eyes were silver and his jet-black hair fell in a braid down his back. Carrying a golden staff and larger than rest, he was easily recognizable as the one in charge.

"Why do you trespass here, Assass`i? You have no God here."

Straightening away from the downed angel, Jazz refused to show any signs of pain from the open wound across his spine as he answered. "I seek an audience with the Fates," he said, seeing no other way around it. He would have to deal with them now he'd been caught. He was good, but this was not his world, and he would most certainly lose a fight here against such odds, although he fully intended to take a few of them out with him.

Silver eyes glanced toward his sword. "Do you hope to kill a being as powerful as a Fate with such a puny weapon?" he asked with a snort of derision.

Jazz dropped his gaze to the floor where the giant's staff rested at his feet before lifting his eyes upward to where the top of the golden weapon ended above the creature's wings.

"I have no need to overcompensate," Jazz answered dryly.

Throwing his head back and exposing a mouth full of sharp pointed teeth, the dark angel roared with laughter. After wiping a tear of mirth from his eye, he slapped Jazz across the shoulder jovially. Jazz's knees nearly buckled from the blow, and the wound that was already knitting closed seeped again, but he stayed upright by force of will.

"Keep your tiny toothpick, Assass`i. I will take you to the place you seek, but you may not thank me for it

51

later."

Flicking his thumb across the lever on his sword, it silently slid back into place inside his sleeve. The downed angel sprang to his feet, wiping imagery dust from his wings.

"Then I shall thank you now," Jazz said with a slight nod of his chin. "I am Jazz."

"Samuel," the dark one replied as he turned and motioned for Jazz to follow. Two more creatures fell in step behind him, causing Jazz to split his attention between memorizing each direction they turned and watching for any signs of attack. Reaching a set of bright red doors, Samuel threw them both wide and strode in.

The three women occupying the room all turned in their direction at the sound of their arrival. The rest of the universe knew the sisters Rowena, Selena, and Karina as the three Fates. All three women were beautiful in an aesthetic way as in it was only skin-deep. They were vastly different in coloration. Rowena's hair was a blazing red and her eyes the color of emeralds. Selena held more of an aristocratic air with her coal black hair and blue eyes. Karina's appearance mimicked the gods' with her golden hair and eyes. All three women were dressed in black satin floor-length dresses that plunged way below the neckline. Jazz was as unmoved by their gorgeous exterior as he was any female. His wife, Cherish, was the only person capable of stirring any emotion in his heart or body. She was his personal gift from his God as a reward for his loyal service. The three women did not seem surprised to see him, despite that fact that his tall solid muscle form, covered in intricate tattoos, clashed vividly against the elegant solid white room.

"I come for Heru," he announced, not bothering with any niceties.

Karina turned her back to him and stared out a nearby window while Rowena let out a snort of derision.

"You think to take a God from this place and yet you offer us nothing in return?" Selena said, sounding practical and establishing herself as the leader of the three. Samuel moved to stand behind her chair, taking up his position as guard.

Jazz never allowed his stoic expression to change. "Exchange," he repeated as if the word was new to him and in a sense, it was. His position as God's greatest warrior afforded him the luxury of absolute power. "Exchange" was not a word he used often. "What sort of exchange did you have in mind?"

Selena tapped her fingers on the table as if considering his question.

"The price of a God as powerful as Heru is high indeed. Jackson Station is your home, is it not?" At

Jazz's nod, Selena flashed a dangerous smile. "There is a family of four living there, a human family, that we would like to add to our collection," she said, pointing toward a nearby window. The sun shone brightly, casting a glittery light throughout the room through the clear pane of glass, and he could see thousands of tiny balls of light floating through the air. He recognized the glowing orbs. Each one was the life spark of a human or a soul as most people knew them.

"You want me to bring you the soul of four of my townsfolk?" he asked, already feeling the heat of his wife's anger despite having yet to do anything wrong.

"Not just any four people. We want Dan and Lena Simmons and their daughter Kera, along with her husband, Weave." Cherish would kill him.

"I cannot allow any harm to befall the ones you have named. They are under my protection."

"We do not wish to harm them," Rowena said before Selena cut off her words with a sharp look.

"As my sister says, we do not mean them harm. It is merely an exchange of souls, one God soul for four human souls. The humans will remain living in your realm, except they will become virtually immortal, as we need them there, and if something should happen to destroy their physical form, then they shall come here instead of reverting to Earth's heavenly realm."

There were hundreds of realms to visit, if you were a God, or if you had been granted special privileges by one, as he had. However, if you were human, you were assigned a specific realm, depending upon several factors, such as your species, the deity to which you paid homage, and whether if you had lived a good life or a bad one. Jazz could not find a reason to decline the bargain, except for the fact that Dan and his family might not wish to live here when they died, or give up their mortality. The tiny detail of Cherish castrating him when he dropped this news was also a factor, but he didn't have a choice.

Selena held her breath as she awaited his decision. She had learned millennia ago never to show how desperate she was to win while bartering a deal.

"You're asking me to take away their free will?" Jazz asked in tone devoid of all emotion. He could have been asking about tomorrow's weather for all the care he showed the loss of four people's afterlife.

"Free will," Karina repeated with a snort of derision, and speaking up for the first time. "There is no such thing, not really, and what do you care? You suffer no human emotions beyond those granted to you, by Earth's God, for your wife."

Selena broke in. "Let's leave it to the flip of a coin, what say you?" Selena asked, conjuring up a golden piece between her fingers. "Tails," she said, showing him that side of the coin. "Heru will remain here with his father and we will pretend this meeting never took place, or heads," she continued, flipping the coin to show the head. "Heru will return with you to the middle ground and you will escort the previously named souls here so we may arrange for their eternal life."

She watched for any hint of indecision to appear upon his face, even though she knew that it would not, and a smile of satisfaction touched her lips when he gave a short nod. With a flick of her thumb, the coin sailed into the air, making several flips. Every eye in the room followed its progress until it came to rest on the floor. Dead silence filled the room as they held a collective breath and leaned forward to learn Heru's fate. A tiny head stared up at the room. It was done. Heru would return to the land of the living and the Safe Haven team would forfeit their souls. Straightening in her seat, Selena met Jazz's gaze. "You may take the son of Geb with you today. However, Samuel will escort you here in three day's time with the four agreed-upon humans. From there, I shall arrange their immortality. My souhaitant shall show you the way to Heru." At the snap of her fingers, Samuel, the young male guardian who served her needs for centuries, moved from his position behind her chair to her side. Samuel's jet-black waist-length ponytail fell over his shoulder as he gave Jazz a slight bow and motioned for him to follow. Jazz nodded to each of them before falling in step behind Samuel. Selena held her spine straight until the last wisps of Jazz's long black coat crossed the threshold, and then she slipped down a notch in her seat.

"You flipped a coin," Rowena said with disbelief coloring each word as the door closed behind Jazz. A wicked smile touched Selena's lips as she scooped up the golden piece from the floor. Angling it toward the light between her thumb and forefinger, she tapped it with the tip of her finger, revealing a head etched on both sides.

"I guess it was a matter of fate," she said wickedly.

*****

Jazz could see every muscle in Heru's body go on high alert as soon as the door to his chamber clicked open. Although he kept his face smooth of all emotion, Jazz noticed the fingers of Heru's right hand clenched tightly, belying his nonchalant stance.

"What's this?" Heru asked, sounding confused as he switched his gaze between Samuel and Jazz. Catching Heru's eye, Jazz gave him a slight nod of approval. He'd hoped Heru would be smart enough to act as if they'd never met.

"It seems you are bartered goods," Samuel answered, and a line formed in Heru's brow as his confusion seemed to become genuine.

"No worries, my friend," Samuel said, slapping

Heru across the shoulder with the same force he had shown Jazz earlier. Heru did not as much as flinch at the blow, impressing Jazz with this strength. Of course, the dark angel was most likely no more than a flea compared to a God.

"You fetched a good price," Samuel reassured him. "Four human souls," he added.

Heru's eyes flashed with anger and Jazz knew in that moment he had made the right decision. Heru would not have willingly traded places with anyone else, proving that he was a good man.

"I'll explain on the way," Jazz told him quietly before switching his attention to Samuel. "Thank you again for your assistance."

"Blah," Samuel said, waving a dismissive hand. "You still should not thank me. This one is an angry one, always breaking things, and attempting escape. I'm happy to be shut of him."

Samuel continued muttering under his breath about ungrateful gods trapped in their rightful place as he led them back to the front room. It was once again filled with mirrors.

"I'll assume you can find your way home from here, Assass`i Jazz," Samuel said as he walked them to the door. At his nod, the dark angel stepped through the closest mirror, sending waves rippling through it like water, before it became solid once more. Now he was alone with Heru, Jazz could feel the anger rolling off him in waves, but Jazz wasn't concerned. Heru's temper didn't hold a candle to Cherish's, and she would be so pissed.

*****

A sharp indrawn breath signaled Jazz's return and in a matter of seconds with a few words that went unheard by Marissa, he cleared the entire room. Marissa barely noticed the others' exit over the beating of her own heart. Her vision darkened around the edges and she felt like she was staring at everything through a tunnel as she caught her first glimpse of Heru. Cloaked from head to toe in black, her golden-eyed God gazed back at her with an expressionless face as if awaiting her reaction.

Relief, shock, and elation all swirled together in her mind leaving her off-balance.

"Heru," she breathed as she stood before realizing her legs wouldn't hold her weight. She sat once more and Heru was across the room in an instant, kneeling at her feet.

"Breathe," he ordered as he cupped her face between his hands. It wasn't until he said the word she realized that her lungs weren't working. She held his steady gaze and took a deep breath while her mind continued to race. His warm touch on her skin told her he was real and the racing of her heart slowed. For a year now, he'd

59

come to her in a ghostlike form while she was awake and joined her dreams at night. However, it had been thousands of years since she'd felt the solid touch of his real hands against her skin. Searching her face, he brushed his thumb along her cheek.

"I've waited for so long," she said, swallowing past her tears and adding, "through so many lifetimes."

Heru drew back and his brow furrowed, showing his confusion. "How long have you been here?"

"This is my twenty-eighth lifetime since you disappeared," she admitted. "I followed you as soon as I could, but it took a few times before I could find a way to stay here without fear of growing old or dying."

Heru opened his mouth as if to say something before closing it again as if she'd left him speechless. Staring over her shoulder, he continued brushing her skin with his fingertips, seemingly unaware of the motion as he fell into his own thoughts. When he met her gaze once more, his were eyes filled with pain.

"I didn't know. If I had only known," he choked out.

"Oh, baby I know," she soothed, sliding off the couch, and wrapping her arms tightly around his shoulders. Burying her nose in the crook of his neck, Marissa inhaled his scent. The smell of sky filled her lungs, and she held back her sob of desperation. She wanted to crawl inside his skin and never leave so they could never be apart again. It was part pleasure and pain finally to hold him again. All of her waiting was at an end, yet she now knew how much she stood to lose and how painful existence was without him. Even though she knew Jazz had done this to rid the world of Rani, she could never repay him for his kindness, and she would kill Rani with her bare hands before she allowed him to steal her heart from her.

CHAPTER FIVE

"Fate will knock you on your ass every time, especially if it sees you running from it."

-The Society of Sinners

Many years ago, Dan Simmons had been known as Geoff Landers. Back then, he worked as a computer programmer and was considered the best hacker in the world. His life had been a comfy one with a lovely wife and two beautiful daughters. All that changed the day he refused to help a well-known terrorist group hack into the government's system. His family had been slaughtered and as far as the world knew, he had died at their side.

In truth, the government he protected gave him a new life, one where he could help others like him, and get the revenge for his family they deserved. A great deal had happened in his life since then. He'd struck out on his own, created Safe Haven, married the woman of his dreams, and had a daughter. In the early days of Safe Haven, he never dreamed that the list of terrorists would grow to include an entire world of supernatural creatures nor that he would one day be facing the fact he would have to become one of them.

Cherish stood toe to toe with Jazz. "How could you do this, Jazz? How could you use our friends like bargaining chips?"

Dan listened to the ongoing argument with half an ear while searching inside himself for the right answer. He wanted to rage or reassure him they would be fine, but he felt nothing. A part of his brain recognized he was in shock, but the rest of his mind refused to admit to such an unmanly reaction to Jazz's pronouncement that their souls had been traded for Heru's. He opened his mouth, unsure of what to say, but Lena beat him to the punch.

"I had a dream once where I was in this hospital and I was wearing one of those awful gowns they give you. This man came into my room, lifted me into his arms, and carried me away. He took me to see all these wonderful places I never even knew that I wanted to see until that moment. I was so amazed by everything, but more at peace than I've ever been in my life."

"You don't have to do this," Jazz told her quietly.

Lena smiled sadly. "I think that I do."

Even the air seemed to hold its breath as Jazz and Lena held each other's gaze. Kera kept her shoulders squared as if prepared for anything while Weave looked almost relieved by Jazz's news. Finally, Jazz gave a short nod and Lena drew in a ragged breath.

"That man was you," Lena said, inclining her head in Jazz's direction. "Of course, it wasn't until I met you I realized the significance of that dream."

At Lena's admission, Dan's mind screeched to a halt before racing off in every direction. With all the questions running through his brain, the one that fell stupidly from his lips was, "What?"

Lena turned in his direction and he realized her eyes were filled with tears. The devastated look on her face shook him more than anything else could have and it went far toward clearing his head. "How long have you known this?" he asked, attempting to keep some of the hurt from his voice.

"Known about Jazz or known they would not let us leave?"

"Well, both," Dan answered. "I mean, you're my wife. Why did you keep this a secret?"

"I knew who Jazz was as soon as we were introduced, but I didn't figure out they wouldn't let us leave until Jazz gave Kera his blood to save her life. Then, a few days ago, I saw Colin's death in the cards and everything fell into place. This has been the plan from the beginning."

"And I ask again, why didn't you say anything?" Dan said, feeling his anger rising.

Lena let out a tiny sound of despair. "How could I tell you that our lives had been maneuvered to this point? How could I tell you that our friend had to choose who would have to live and need die to get us here? But most of all, how could I tell you I knew Colin would die? I did nothing to stop it, because it was meant to be, and we have no real control over fate. I knew that you would never look at me the same."

Kera had been sitting with her hand over her mouth throughout the entire conversation, but she finally broke at Lena's last words. "Oh, Mom," she cried, jumping to her feet and coming to her side. "It is such a burden. I understand."

As Kera wrapped an arm around Lena's shoulders, tucking her into her side, Jazz stepped forward and handed Lena a sealed white envelope.

"Colin left this for you," he explained.

Her hands shook as she reached for it and tears streamed silently down her face as she tore it open pulling out the note from inside. Smoothing out the page across her knees, she continued running her hands across the folds as if removing the creases would somehow fix everything.

"I can't," she finally choked out and Kera gently took the letter from her lap.

"Lena," Kera read aloud. "My first service is to protect the world and death is my final assignment. Please don't hang onto the guilt I know that you are feeling. The ability to see it happening didn't change my fate. You will never understand how much comfort you brought me in my final days because I know that I am not facing the end alone. You are here with me in heart." If hearts make a sound as they break, then that's how Dan would have described the one that fell from Lena's lips as Kera continued reading Colin's letter.

"I am but one warrior capable of saving few while you are an angel of mercy bringing comfort and peace to many. I hope I can make you as proud of me in death as I have been of you in life. Ever with my head held high, Colin."

Lena seemed to turn inside herself as if having gone numb to it all. He'd been so blind, Dan realized with outstanding clarity. Of course, Lena would know everything before it happened and Kera was right. It was a horrible burden.

"You should have told me. You didn't have to do this alone," Dan said.

Lena shook her head slowly. "You're such a wonderful man," she said, sounding as if all the energy had been drained from her as her red-rimmed eyes met his. "You would have done anything within your power to keep Colin alive. You would have never accepted that it was his time." And she'd been forced to handle it completely alone. Lena cried so hard she could no longer speak and Jazz took over as Kera hugged her tightly.

"The four of you are unique in your gifts and unlike

any other humans alive. Lena with her gift of sight, Dan with his ability to keep our people safe, Weave the friend of God, and Kera as the only person capable of keeping Weave on his path. Plus," Jazz paused and glanced down at his feet for a moment as if gathering himself before looking back up. "You are our friends and we don't want you to die. Colin knew his death would set into motion the events that would ensure your eternal life."

Weave cleared his throat and stood. "Speaking of friends, I'm going to go check on our guests and see if they are still with us or if they've gone on to their cabin. I'm sure they're ready to spend some time together and may be waiting on final word from us."

He'd shown the least reaction to the news and Dan wondered what was going on inside Weave's head. He almost made it to the door before Jazz reached out and touched his arm, bringing him to a halt. The gesture alone came as a huge shock since Jazz never willingly touched anyone other than his wife.

"I'm sorry," Jazz said, further surprising Dan, but Weave only shifted from foot to foot, seeming uncomfortable with the conversation.

"Naw, man," Weave said with a shake of his head. "Naw," he repeated, running his hand over his head. "We both know I never had a shot at Heaven," he said, leaving the room before anyone could argue. Maybe that was the gist of it, Dan decided. Perhaps the things they had all done in the name of justice had only been right to their own minds while in truth they were all beyond forgiveness.

*****

The years of pain they could have missed weighed heavy on Heru's mind as they traveled to the cabin where they would be staying. As the tiny wooden structure came into view, Heru felt the tug of magical wards sliding over his skin, but even that was not enough to pull him from his thoughts. It wasn't until the door closed behind him and he stared at the sparsely decorated front room of the chalet he could come back to the present. What little furniture the place possessed appeared faded and worn, but the cabin seemed clean. Marissa crossed the room and tossed her keys on a nearby coffee table.

"What is this place?"

At his question, Marissa gave a tiny shrug. "Cherish lived here before marrying Jazz. It's not much, but it's well protected."

Lodgings that belonged to a friend, instead of one rented for private use, meant the possibility of disturbance, and that was a thought that did not set well with Heru. Reaching behind him, he turned the lock on the door. He wasn't feeling very tolerant of interruptions at the moment. At the sound of the lock clicking in place, Marissa wrung her hands together nervously before shoving them behind her back and her face flushed. A majority of the room was cast in shadows with the exception of the one lone lamp that had been lit in expectation of their arrival, but his vision was perfect in the dark, and the color in her cheeks stood out bright. He wondered if it was from embarrassment or arousal. She wore a short pink dress that matched the color of her lips and left her arms bare. As Heru's feet carried him across the room, he imagined how easy it would be to slip the dress from her body. They had several things they needed to talk about, but it would not happen tonight. They both knew it. He watched her every movement, taking in each detail. He absorbed her physical presence as if he was a drowning man and she was his only oxygen. The sweet smell of her perfume filled his lungs. The need to touch her, to know that she was real, was almost painful in its intensity. When he stood toe to toe with her, Marissa pressed her hand to her stomach, drawing in a deep breath.

"If you could see the way you're looking at me," she said.

Closing the final inches between them, Heru pried her hand away from her stomach before linking his fingers through hers.

"What would I see?" he asked, curious to know.

"Hunger," she answered, sounding breathless.

Instead of responding, he lifted their linked hands to his mouth, and kissed the tip of each of her fingers as he held her eyes with his. He drew in a deep breath. "Everything is so much more here," he explained, as he swiped his tongue across the pulse at her wrist before closing his lips over it and sucking lightly. With a tug, he pulled her an inch closer. Dipping his head, he trailed kisses up to the inside her elbow. "Every smell is stronger," he said, inhaling the scent of her skin. "Every taste has more flavor," he said as he placed another open-mouthed kiss upon her arm. Continuing his exploration, he moved to her collarbone, and spoke against her skin. "Every touch is more intense."

Marissa's free hand found its way beneath the hem of his shirt and she brushed her fingertips along the line of his abs. He sucked in a hiss between his teeth at the touch. He'd not been exaggerating. In the heavens, everything was muted, but here, even the air seemed heavier on his skin. Chill bumps broke out over his body as her touch traveled to his hardened nipple. His shirt rose higher the further she went until most of his torso was bared to her. Marissa kept her eyes locked on her hand's progression, but he couldn't look away from her face. He knew the hypersensitivity would leave him after a few days, but for now, he could feel her every breath and heartbeat. He could almost taste her lust and it heightened his own. He wanted to play witness to the entire thing. He wanted to memorize the expressions that crossed her face and savor them forever. Her clear blue eyes lifted to his. "Will you take this off?" she asked, tugging on his shirt.

He pulled the shirt over his head without hesitation. His mind screamed for him to take her now, but he held himself in check as his dick screamed in denial. The look on her face as she stared at his bare chest was almost his undoing, and he cast a frantic look around the room in an attempt to keep from jumping on her like a starving dog. Instead of finding a distraction, he pictured all the different ways he could take her. The table looked sturdy enough to hold them and the couch was the exact height needed to bend her over. Running a hand over his face, he fought for control. When she leaned in, sealing her lips over his nipple, he sucked in his breath. The sound of her heart beating at the base of her throat exploded in his ears and he shook his head to rid himself of it.

"Fuuuckk," he groaned, snatching her off her feet, and causing her to giggle. "Where's the bedroom? I refuse to take you like an animal." Marissa curled into his chest and sighed, pointing toward the open door to his left. With a few quick strides, he came to the edge of the bed. Bracing his knee on the mattress, he slowly lowered Marissa onto it before following her down and covering her with his body. Nothing else about the room registered in his brain. The only thing he could see, smell, and feel was Marissa. A tiny smile hovered on her lips, and her eyes glittered with happiness. Holding her gaze, he moved in, memorizing every detail of her expression as it changed from humor to longing. When their lips met, he heard a growl, and realized the noise had come from him.

The flavor of exotic spices exploded across Marissa's taste buds as Heru's tongue stoked hers. Frustration clawed at her belly as he kept his touch light. She knew that he was attempting to go slowly, but she didn't want slowly. The harder she tried to move against his body in an attempt to spur him into action, the tighter his hold became, leaving her immobilized. The sheer size of his body amazed her. In her dreams and memories, he wasn't this huge. The flat pads of his chest spread wide, dipping deeply in the center. The hard lines of muscle in his stomach contracted against her and she dug her fingernails into his back in reprisal for his torment. His back tightened and rippled beneath her touch as he reached down, slipping the hem of her dress upwards. Sinking her teeth into his bottom lip, she then ran her tongue over it in apology before deepening the kiss once more. As he reached the edge of her panties, her sex pulsed in anticipation, but he simply curled his fingers around the material and held on. A whimper bubbled from her chest and the sound of fabric ripping rent the air as the satin of her underwear lost the match against his strength. She knew in that moment that his arousal matched her own and she wanted to see it unleashed. Tearing her mouth away, she ran her teeth along the column of his neck while grappling with his

72

pants. Her clothes hindered her movements as Heru pulled down the straps, freeing her breasts. His tongue flattened over her nipple and the air left her lungs in a whoosh. Their panting filled the air, but a surge of triumph rushed through her veins when she worked his pants past his hips. Heru's body was evenly proportioned and his cock was no exception. Long and thick, it felt heavy pressing against her core. Every deep pull of his mouth at her nipple went straight to her center.

"Heru," she begged. "I need you."

Lifting his head, he stared down at her. With his face flushed, eyes shining, and lips parted on a breath, he was by far the sexiest thing she'd ever seen. His hand slipped between their bodies. Taking himself in hand, he rubbed the tip of his cock over her clit, causing another whimper to fall from her lips.

"Please, Heru," she pled.

He probed at her entrance and groaned as he inched inside. "Ever as you command," he said, covering her mouth and swallowing her cry as he surged forward. The walls of her canal stretched wide, but he was large and even as wet as she was, her body took a moment to adjust. Instead of pulling out, Heru pivoted his hips, causing a friction between them. Gripping his ass between her hands, she moved against him, seeking more of the pleasure he offered. A pulse beat in her clit and as his cock slipped in and out of her, it only added to the sensation. She could hear a mewling coming from her throat, but she incapable of stopping it. Bracing his hands against the bed beside her head, Heru pulled back. He stared down at her through lowered lids, and the sight of his face mesmerized her. His lips were swollen from her biting kisses and they were slightly parted on a breath. Witnessing how turned on he was in that moment added strength to the orgasm that suddenly snagged her in its grasp. "Damn," he whispered, holding her gaze as she rode out every wave. Squeezing him tight with her inner muscles, she milked him into release, savoring his every moan and clutching the moment to her chest for safekeeping.

Discarding their rumpled clothing, Heru tossed them on the floor and tugged the covers over their sweat-covered bodies to protect them from the night's chill. Exhaustion overcame her, sweeping her away as soon as he curled his warm body around hers.

CHAPTER SIX

He may as well have died. He was every bit as gone from Marissa's life as if she had been forced to scatter his ashes across the sea, and her heart knew only a deep emptiness where he used to be. How could she go on living without him? It was too hard. What choice did she have? Every night, she watched the sky and searched her dreams for any hint of his of presence, but each morning she awoke to a fresh wave of pain. Heru was gone.

-Excerpt from the Legend of Fire and Water

Marissa's eyes shot open, and for a moment the fear it had all been a dream left her paralyzed, but the warmth of Heru's hip touching hers calmed her racing heart. He was sitting up, but he had not moved away from her side, and she'd never been more thankful for anything. The moonlight streaming through the nearby window seemed to hold him in thrall, leaving Marissa full reign to feast on the muscled expanse of his back. A back riddled with scars. Deep white lines and raised ridges crisscrossed every single inch of skin. She was amazed that she had not felt them earlier, but her mind had been fogged with lust. Her heart ached at the thought of what he must have endured over the years.

"Gods don't scar," she said as she slid her hand along his spine.

She felt his shrug. "The fallen ones do."

Running her fingers over the longest one, Marissa heard the question fall from her lips before she could stop it from happening. "What was it like when you first came here?" She had time to grow and adjust, but he had been thrust into the mortal realm with no warning.

Heru glanced back over his shoulder at her and his golden gaze seemed to glimmer in the otherwise darkened room. "You don't want to know this," he told her quietly.

"You're right; I don't," she admitted. "But I think that I need to know."

Heru looked away. "It was cold," he answered, and Marissa almost stopped him then. It was the worst sort of fate for a star. She held her tongue and Heru continued without showing an ounce of emotion. "My body shook uncontrollably from it and I thought I would never be warm again. I raged and screamed. I called my father's name and begged for help. Several times I tried swimming as far out into the Sea as I could, hoping I could reach you and hoping that I'd drown when I could not. I spent several weeks simply staring at the horizon until my eyes were so dry they felt like they were filled with shards of glass, but I didn't want to miss spotting you there."

She felt sick. Squeezing her eyes closed against the pain, she forced herself to remain quiet in fear he wouldn't tell her the rest, and when he paused, she wondered if he would. With her fingers pressed against his back, she felt him take a steadying breath and when he spoke once more, he didn't sound as lifeless. "When I finally accepted that I would never see you again, I became truly desperate, and drew a pentagram in the sand. I wanted to forget," he admitted. A tear slid from the corner of her eye, and as if he felt the tear fall, Heru whipped around to face her.

"I'm sorry," Marissa said.

In a motion almost too quick for the eye, Heru threw a leg over her hips, straddling her body, boxing her in with his arms, and pinning her to the bed with the sheet.

"Why?" Heru asked on a growl.

The look of anger on Heru's face made her want to turn her head, but she held his gaze steady, refusing to back down. "You know why," she whispered.

"Do you regret loving me?" he demanded.

Marissa shook her head. "You know that I could never."

"You said that this is your twenty-eighth life. Do you remember each one?"

Marissa nodded in answer.

"You suffered each day alone while I chose to forget. You willingly left all you knew behind for an uncertain life; so I ask again, why are you sorry?"

More tears burned for release, but Marissa refused to let them fall. "You know why," she repeated.

"Perhaps you should refresh my memory. And may the Gods have mercy on you should you decide to confess regretting me," he added, sounding angrier than she'd ever heard him sound before.

"Because I wished for your heart," she admitted.

Lowering his head, Heru chuckled as he touched his lips to her ear. "I will let you in on a secret," he whispered. "It does you no good to wish for that in which you already own."

His warm breath against her skin caused a shiver of anticipation to race down her spine. "I set your fate in motion that night," she pressed on, refusing to allow him to dismiss her hand in things so easily.

"Mhmm, yes you did," he purred, kissing the column of her neck. She sighed as she realized that she'd already lost the battle.

"You're not going to let me take any of the blame, are you?"

Heru hid his smile. "I'll let you have all the blame you want. What should I hold you responsible for first?" he asked, nuzzling her throat. "Let's see, it's your fault I'm so turned on right now." Rolling his hips, Heru made sure she felt the erection pressing into her skin. "Yep, it's definitely your doing I'm hard as a rock. I mean, that sort of thing could cause a permanent limp."

Marissa's body shook with suppressed laughter as he intended. Prying the sheet from between them, Heru shifted to the side and stared down the line of her body, allowing his hunger to grow. Trailing his fingers along her skin, he watched in fascination as a line of chill bumps rose beneath his touch. Meeting her eyes once more, he confessed, "It's all your fault that I'm gloriously happy."

Her laughter died on a gasp as he traced a circle around her nipple, and her knees fell open. A pulse beat in his cock as her hand fluttered to her stomach before drifting downward. Not daring to breathe, he watched its progression, and a spike of disappointment shot through him when she stopped short of her mound.

Covering her hand with his, he guided her fingers to her wet folds.

"Touch her for me," he begged. "I want to watch."

Resting his head beneath her breast, he listened to the steady beat of her heart and drew her scent into his lungs. Two of her fingers disappeared inside her before reappearing soaked with her juices. Using the moisture, Marissa circled her clit. He palmed his cock unable to resist his body's call. She moved restlessly against her own touch and he matched her pace. Stroking his shaft, he took in the sounds of her moans and the sight of her gleaming sex. The need to orgasm ripped at his insides, and when her muscles tightened beneath his cheek, his balls drew up tight as if her pleasure was his own. When she jerked, an orgasm took him by surprise, and he rode out the crest until the final drop of his semen covered her stomach.

With one appetite assuaged, another roared to life, taking its place, and he ground his back teeth against it. Despite the roar of her racing heartbeat, he cleaned her skin with the sheet before kicking it to the floor. Curling his body around hers, he allowed the air to dry the sweat that lingered on their skin. He would allow nothing to ruin this moment, not even the needs of his body. The red haze in his vision receded, taking the tightness in his chest along with it. Praying the hunger wouldn't return, he leaned in for one last lingering kiss before sleep carried her away from him.

"I burn hotter for you than any star in the sky," he whispered against her hair.

"My love is deeper than the sea," she replied, sounding more asleep than awake.

His eyes fell closed and his throat tightened. Only the Gods knew how he longed to hear those words on her lips again. "You are the only good thing about me," he confessed, but the dream world had already claimed her.

Heru waited until Marissa's breathing deepened further before moving away. There was not a doubt in his mind they'd been given Cherish's old cabin on purpose and a quick check of the window proved him right. Searching the room, he found the remote that controlled the blackout blinds, and he slid them all into place before rejoining Marissa. The last thing he wanted was for her to wake up snuggled up to a pile of ashes. That would be hard to explain.

*****

Pain sliced through him, and he gripped the doorframe for support as his knees threatened to buckle beneath him. Heru squeezed his eyes shut as the room spun until things righted themselves once more. Once he was sure he could move without landing on his ass, he headed straight for the bathroom, following the sound of the running water. Stumbling inside, the steam from the shower and the sweet smell of Marissa's body wash hit him in the face. A huge part of him wanted to rip back the shower curtain and join her inside. He could almost feel the steady beat of the water against his back and the weight of Marissa in his arms as he pictured her legs wrapped around his waist. It would be so easy to take her against the wall. The desire to feel her tight wet heat surrounding his dick almost had him doing just that, but the pain churning in his gut kept him in check.

"I need to run over to see Jazz," he called through the curtain.

Poking her head out, Marissa's brow furrowed as she eyed him closely. "Is everything okay?" The concern in her voice caused his guilt to skyrocket. Unexpectedly, every sound in the room cranked up a notch, leaving him disoriented. Gritting his back teeth, he gave her a short nod, praying she didn't notice.

"Give me a few minutes to finish up and I'll go with you," she offered, but he waved it off.

"I'll only be gone for a few minutes," he promised her. "I'll be back before you're dressed." Her face fell at his words.

Shit. She looked disappointed, and he fucking hated himself for it. He was trying so hard not to fuck things up. He'd cut his right arm off before he let her see the evil bastard he'd become over the years.

"Promise me you won't get dressed," he growled.

A mischievous glint lit her eyes. "Only if you hurry," she teased.

That smile punched him in the chest and his eyes locked onto a bead of water that ran down from her collarbone before sliding over her breast. Her nipples hardened beneath his stare and he lifted his gaze to hers. A slight flush appeared high on her cheeks as he leaned toward her.

"Don't get dressed," he ordered as he claimed her

mouth for a hard kiss. Their tongues met briefly before he pulled away. He left while she was still dazed and he could still walk.

By the time Heru made it to Jazz's house, he was ready to collapse, the last of his strength depleted. Luckily, Cherish knew what he needed immediately, and he was sucking down his third bag of blood in a matter of moments. It wasn't until he was on his fourth he felt self-conscious under their stares.

"I don't understand," Cherish said finally. "Why didn't you drink from Marissa? She is your other half, so it isn't forbidden."

"I can't risk her becoming like me," he answered, tossing the bag in the trash.

"I don't think it's possible for you to spread a curse," Jazz said with a shrug. "And you're too important to allow your strength to wane."

"I couldn't live with myself if I somehow tainted her blood."

Jazz shook his head at Heru's confession. "You must have fed from millions of mortals over the centuries."

"I doubt that," he said, laughing. "Most tainted Vampires keep blood slaves. They turn a mortal to keep at their side to feed from instead of having to hunt for new prey," he explained. "Especially since the world has not always been so over populated. Something I believe your wife knows a great deal about," he added, turning his attention to Cherish. Her hand fluttered to her neck and a low growl sounded from deep in Jazz's chest, but Heru waved off the threat.

"I can smell the difference in your blood, but do not concern yourself over it. Your secret is safe with me. After all, who am I to judge?"

Cherish cleared her throat twice as if it could clear away her shock before she spoke. "I appreciate your silence."

Jazz's voice held a stiff note as he steered the subject back on course. "Have you ever created a blood slave?" Heru noted the fact that "blood slave" came out of Jazz's mouth sounding like he was chewing on glass, but that wasn't surprising, considering the guy's wife used to be one.

Heru shook his head in answer. "They were always provided to me by Ranihura. It served a double purpose for him to do so. He controlled my food supply while also having a spy for my home."

"Surely you have fed from more than blood slaves over the years," Jazz noted.

Heru knew that Jazz was attempting to lead him to his own conclusion about something, but he could not see what it was.

"Of course," he admitted.

"Have you ever left a taint behind?"

Heru let out a mirthless laugh. "I think I left one very famously behind: Pharaoh Hor-aha."

Jazz's expression never changed, but oddly Heru felt as if Jazz was disappointed in him somehow, as if he was missing a key point in the discussion.

"Let's try this another way," Jazz said, changing tactics. "Do you know, in theory, how a blood slave or tainted Vampire is created?" he asked.

Feeling a bit irritated that Jazz would not come out and say whatever point he wanted to get across, Heru snapped. "Of course, I do. A tainted Vampire would need to drain their victim until right before their heart stopped, and then feed them," he trailed off as realization struck. Jazz smiled.

"Wait," Heru said slowly. "When I bit the Pharaoh—"

"You did nothing more than piss him off," Jazz said, cutting him off.

"I don't understand," he said plainly. "The Pharaoh is cursed the same as I have been, and even Kim has said that I caused her father's transformation. I never considered it to be otherwise since he was the only person I have ever bitten while in leopard form."

Jazz shook his head. "Kim believes what her father has allowed her to accept as the truth. You were the excuse he'd been searching for to reveal himself to her. In fact, he sold his soul many years earlier to Samael for the power to bring peace to his people. He mistakenly believed he would not have to pay for his end of the bargain since he is not of the Christian faith. That is also the reason I am forbidden to help him."

Anger rolled off Heru in waves. He'd tortured himself for years, believing that he was responsible for the Pharaoh's fate.

"If it makes you feel any better, he felt a great deal of guilt over turning his back on you, and spent most his life attempting to atone for it by taking in other lost souls," Jazz said, attempting to soothe Heru's temper.

"In truth, it does not make me feel any better," Heru shot back, feeling the muscles in his face tense with the effort it took to keep from lashing out at the world.

Jazz shrugged. "At any rate, you are cursed, not contagious."

Heru's shoulders relaxed a bit as the worry over harming Marissa fell away before another one took its place. He shifted in his seat and rubbed his palms over the knees of his jeans nervously. "There is another problem with me feeding from Marissa," he admitted and Jazz raised an eyebrow in question.

"She doesn't know that I'm cursed."

Both of Jazz's eyebrows shot to his hairline at Heru's confession. "That is a problem."

*****

The silence inside the cabin left Marissa uneasy. It was strange because her own home was every bit as empty, but here it seemed more isolated than peaceful. Tugging a t-shirt over her head, Marissa decided Heru would have to be happy with her partially dressed and minus the underwear. As hard as she tried, she couldn't walk around nude. Plus, as fifteen minutes turned into thirty, her apprehension grew.

Trailing from room to room, she checked each one, hoping to set her mind at ease, and questions crowded her brain. How long did it take to get to Jazz's house? How long would it take to get back? Finding each room empty and no reason for the alarm bells that were screaming in her head, Marissa busied herself with the math as she headed for the kitchen. If it took ten minutes to get there, ten to get back, and he spent ten minutes talking, then he would be back at any second. Shaking herself, Marissa realized she been standing inside the open door of the refrigerator and staring inside with no real plan. As she spotted a carton of eggs, her stomach growled, and she sent out a whisper of thanks to whoever had stocked up for their arrival. Moving from the fridge to the cabinets, she went in search of the pots and pans. She could see the handle of a black cast iron skillet sticking out underneath a couple of pans inside the drawer beneath the stove. Snagging the handle, she yanked, sending the flat pans flying. The loud clanging bounced off the walls.

"AHA," she cried victoriously, holding the skillet above her head as she stood. A cry of surprise replaced her triumph. She clutched the pan closer to her chest as her eyes landed on the man standing only a few feet from her. He had appeared without a sound. The smell of rotting flesh packed her lungs, causing her nose to burn and her stomach to churn. Her mind refused to work as fear and shock fogged her brain. The beat of her heart now filled the once silent house. He made no move toward her, but she could sense the evil intent rolling from his body as sure as he was strangling the life from her.

His paper-white skin made his black eyes with no discernible sclera seem all the more ominous, and a slight red glow illuminated the center of them. He wasn't a large man, possibly only five-nine, but she did not doubt his power.

"You know me," he stated, and his voice came out so deep she felt as if the devil had spoken. She shook her head even though she had an idea of who he was. She refused to give him a name. He smiled, showing a set of pointed teeth.

"Smart girl," he cooed.

His nostrils flared as he inhaled deeply. "Fresh sea air with a hint of magic," he said as his eyelids lowered, appearing almost lustful. A chill broke out over her skin at his look and she swallowed down her bile. "Your flesh must be delicious."

A shiver began deep inside her and moved into all of her limbs. She realized there was no escape and she would die. Rani stepped closer, moving slowly as if savoring the moment, and she backed away until the counter bit into the flesh of her back. A sound between a roar and a growl rent the air, freezing the demon's approach. One second Rani was inches from her, and the next he was flying through the air before landing safely on his feet across the room in a crouch.

"Holy shit," Marissa screeched as she caught sight of the creature capable of such a sound. A gigantic leopard stalked the perimeter of the kitchen, keeping his eyes trained upon Rani. A demon had kept her frozen in her tracks, but the sight of the huge wild animal had her scurrying away. Marissa decided if she lived through this, she would analyze her reactions later, but with leopard and demon blocking her exit, the only way was up. In the blink of an eye, she was on top of the counter, holding the frying pan out in front of her, and silently daring anything to attack.

"It's a fucking cat and cats can climb. What the hell

was I thinking?" she asked the room in general, past the point of caring she was talking to herself. At her words, the giant cat in question cast a glance in her direction before turning back to its prey. Rani kept his eyes locked on the beast as if bracing for an attack.

Crouching low, the wild cat sprang. Two feet from the demon, and hanging in mid-air, the leopard transformed into Heru before landing within striking distance of Rani. With a tilt of his head and one last malevolent glance in her direction, Rani disappeared.

Heru's body heaved with each breath, but she couldn't decide if it was due to the exertion or pure rage. Weave and Kera appeared in the doorway, skidding to halt, and breathing heavily as if they'd run all the way there.

"The wards were breached," Weave said, sounding out of breath before finding himself hanging by the neck, and a foot off the floor. Squeezing his fingers around Weave's throat, Heru's eyes changed from gold to iridescent blue and large fangs showed as he spoke.

"What is wrong with you, human? I could have killed you." He emphasized his point by giving Weave a tiny shake.

"Let him go," Kera cried, reaching for Heru's arm, but as soon as her fingers contacted Heru's skin, she screamed. It came from deep inside and curdled the blood as if she was enduring the worst form of torture.

Leaping backward away from her touch, Heru dropped Weave to the floor.

"Never touch me again, Seer," Heru growled. "And you," he added, taking a few long strides coming to a stop before Marissa. "Were you going to fucking stand there and let him kill you?" Heru barked as he pried the frying pan from her numb fingers. She caught a glimpse of fangs still peeking out as he spoke.

"Holy shit," she heard herself say again through the haze of her shock.

"Next time, use your fucking magic, Marissa."

"What's happened to you?" she asked and her teeth chattered.

He knew he was being an ass, but he couldn't stop. She'd almost died, and he was so fucking pissed off that he couldn't see straight.

"Goddamn it. Don't ever scare me like that again," he said, plucking her from the counter top.

Weave kneeled next Kera on the floor. She was sitting up and had stopped screaming, but her face had lost all color.

"What the fuck is going on here?" Weave demanded, sounding exactly like a man who'd almost had his windpipe crushed.

"You wait your goddamn turn," Heru snarled at him. Strolling into their bedroom, he kept Marissa clutched to his chest. He kicked the door closed behind him and carried her to their bed like a child. She was shaking so hard that he could hear it and her fear soothed away some of his anger. Despite her inner strength, it was unlikely she had ever encountered such evil before, and this was exactly what he had wanted to keep from her. Climbing onto the bed, he leaned his back against the headboard and settled her into his lap. She kept a tight grip on his t-shirt as if it was her only hold on reality.

"What did you do to Kera?" she asked, sounding only slightly calmer.

"Unlike Lena, who sees visions in dreams and deciphers the cards, Kera receives hers through touch. Her human mind cannot endure what I have been through," he explained.

Marissa sucked in a choked breath. "What's been done to you?" she whispered against his chest.

How was he supposed to answer that one? What hadn't happened to him? He brushed his knuckles up and down her back, trying to decide where he should start. He tried to see the past, but all he could see was the corner of the room where his eyes remained glued.

"Jazz said that you were a slave. I guess I should have questioned how a demon enslaved a God, even a fallen one, but I didn't want to think of you suffering," she said, her voice still shaking, showing her distress. She must have realized he didn't want to explain. It was another reminder of why he loved her. Something horrible happened to her only moments earlier, and despite her chattering teeth and obvious shock, she worried over his anguish. She deserved to know what she was getting into with him.

"They didn't lock me in the Hall of the Gods to keep me from you," he admitted. "They did it to protect the world from me. There, I don't need to fight the hunger and the light doesn't burn my skin. Here, somewhere along the way, I stopped, shit, I don't know," he said, running a hand over his head in aggravation. "Caring about what was considered wrong, I guess."

"Have you killed people?" she asked quietly, and he felt his grip tighten around her, as if he held her tightly enough, then she could never hate him.

"That wasn't a fair question," she said before he could answer. "You were a soldier of the sky when we met. I knew you were a warrior charged with keeping the heavens safe."

As much as he wanted to let her believe that the life he lived as a soldier was the same as the things he'd done as a taint, he couldn't live that lie. Not with her.

Steeling himself against seeing her love turn to hatred, he touched her chin and tilted her head back. Looking down into her eyes, he felt his chest tighten.

"I--" he began, but she surged upward, cutting off his words as she licked the seam of his lips. He immediately opened for her, savoring her kiss and recognizing her acceptance for the gift it was. As she stroked his tongue with her own, she shifted until she was straddling his legs. Pulling away slightly, she pressed her forehead to his. "You survived. Gods, I do not care how you did it so long as you're here with me."

She left him speechless with her words. She always floored him with her love. It was so fucking unfair that she always settled when it came to him. He wanted to be more than the flame that would engulf her, a ghost with nothing to offer, or a curse with no cure. Pulling away, she buried her nose in the crook of his neck.

"I'm allergic to cats," she joked.

Heru threw back his head and laughed, feeling lighter than he had in years. "I'll find you some pills," he promised, wiping his eyes. The fact she wasn't wearing anything under her shirt slowly sank into his brain. He explored that further, but a knock on the bedroom door froze his fingers on the hem of her shirt.

***

Rani's rage knew no bounds, and he recognized the time had come for another demonstration of his displeasure. He'd underestimated a few things, he could admit that to himself. However, the things from which this shithole town drew strength would also be their downfall.

The ancient Vampire in Martinique had merely been a welcoming gift. Despite his love for a bit of revenge, he had not intended to draw this out. When, he first set his sights on the Goddess of the Sea, he'd thought to kill her quickly, and be done with the matter. Unfortunately, he found Marissa already under Heru's protection and somehow the Society had been forewarned of his presence.

Although the ancient, Colin, admittedly had been more of a rage killing, since he couldn't reach Marissa, it had given him an unexpected piece of a puzzle. He fancied himself a connoisseur of scents and he remembered each one. There had been a hint of fragrance that lingered upon Colin, and it tickled the back of his mind, attempting to draw forth a memory. It wasn't until he'd been forced to flee Heru, once again without his prize, that the same aroma caught his attention. It saturated his pores as it carried on the wind and he followed its trail. Staring through the window of the house, he couldn't believe he had not recognized the scent earlier. It was a Seer. A smile of pure pleasure tugged at the corners of his mouth. Their strength and weakness lie within the hands of a human. It was too delicious.

*****

Lena's cards had gone untouched the entire day, and

that was something that worried Dan more than anything else did. It had been years since that had happened. Their house wasn't the same, and he hated it. Every struggle and hardship they'd encountered over the years they'd faced head-on together. This was different. Instead of standing as a united front, it stood between them, threatening to tear them apart.

"What if we said 'no'?" he asked, giving voice to the question that had been plaguing him all day. Lena was staring off into space and she jumped at the sound of his voice as if she'd forgotten he was there.

"What?"

He moved to sit next to her on the couch and linked his fingers through hers.

"I said, what if we say 'no,'" he repeated. "We could leave here and start a new life somewhere."

A wisp of a smile touched her lips, and he caught a spark of the old Lena in her eyes.

"Is that what you want?"

He shrugged at her question. "I don't know," he answered honestly. "I'm simply looking at our options. What do the cards say will happen if we leave here?" he asked, hoping to kick her out of the black mood that was surrounding her. Unfortunately, it seemed to have the opposite effect as she closed off from him once more.

"If you choose to leave here, then I'll go with you," she said, avoiding his question. Instead of backing down, her withdrawal drove him forward. "But what do the cards say?" he pressed, and her face hardened.

"Whatever you choose, I'll be at your side, but we must make this decision without that. I'm never touching those cards again."

He could hear the conviction in her voice and it shattered his heart. There had always been a spark inside Lena that made her who she was. This shadow he was looking at wasn't her. Some of the devastation he felt over watching her slip away must have shown on his face.

"I don't want to see anymore," she confessed.

This was his fault, he realized with a sudden burst of clarity. He should have forced his way into her thoughts, but instead he looked the other way at some point over the years. There had been a time when he'd needed to understand every odd utterance that fell from her lips, but somewhere along the way, he'd stopped paying attention. He'd always seen himself as strong, but he realized now he was brute force, and she was their strength.

"Did I break us?" he asked, wanting her deny it, and fearing that she wouldn't.

"A person can see too much, know too much," she

began, but a loud knock at the front door cut off her words.

Growling over the interruption, Dan stormed to the door and threw it wide.

"I'd like to speak to you both," Jazz said without preamble.

"Saved by the devil," Dan muttered as he stepped back, waving Jazz inside. However, Jazz froze mid-step, staring over Dan's shoulder, and tensing as if ready to strike.

"Funny you should mention me," a deep voice taunted at his back. Jazz leapt inside as Dan spun to face his intruder, but they were both too late. The demon was gone before Dan could focus on the spot where he had been. Death's scent lingered on the air. Dan watched in horror as blood seeped, slowly at first, from a red line across Lena's throat. Meeting his eyes, she opened her mouth, but no sound escaped as she slipped from the couch and onto the floor. A roar of denial rang in his ears, but he was unaware it came from him. Time seemed to slow and his feet turned heavy as he ran toward her. Dropping to his knees at her side, warm moisture seeped through his jeans as they soaked up her blood. The ground shook, unbalancing him as a fiery ball of light burst through the ceiling. The explosion knocked Dan on his ass and sent him flying back across the room. The impact kicked up a cloud of dust that blocked everything from sight. As the air cleared, Dan spotted a huge dark angel, kneeled on one knee, and with his weight balanced on one of his fists. He leaned over Lena's body, protecting her from the falling debris.

The surrounding floor was cracked and splintered from the impact of his landing. His silver gaze scanned the room as if searching for any hint of lingering danger. Catching sight of Jazz, he nodded. Scooping Lena from the floor, and into his arms, the dark angel cradled her lovingly against his massive chest as he stood. With his wings spread wide, he seemed to fill every inch of the room.

"I told you that toothpick was useless," he told Jazz. "Three days, Assass'i, that was all that was required of you. Do not fail us again."

In the blink on an eye and a flash of light, the angel shot back through the hole in the ceiling, taking Lena with him.

Everything happened so fast that Dan could not react, but the puddle of blood covering the floor spurred him into action. Snatching the Tarot cards from the table, he stuffed them into his back pocket. He grabbed two handfuls of Jazz's shirt and pulled him forward. Pure rage fueled his strength as he dragged Jazz nose to nose with him.

"You take me to her now," he demanded, hearing the threat of death in his own words.

CHAPTER SEVEN

A golden light appeared in the distance and she could see the shadow of a man in the center of it. The Sea Goddess rushed toward him with hope building in her chest. Once she was close enough to see him fully, her eyes filled with tears. It was an older version of the man she loved and she recognized him immediately as the eyes were the same. "My lord," she whispered, bowing her head in reverence of his position, but he lifted her chin to meet his red-rimmed eyes. They mimicked the pain she carried in her heart.

"My son is gone," Geb announced, and the heartbreak in his words ripped away the last of her hope. The tears that threatened to fall upon seeing him made good on their word as they slipped down her cheeks.

Opening his arms wide, she stepped into his embrace, and accepted what comfort he could offer. The warmth of his chest against her cheek only emphasized how alone she now was.

"A father can only dream of having someone love their child as you have loved mine," he whispered against her hair.

"I shall never be whole again," she vowed.

-Excerpt taken from The Legend of Fire and Water

Heru waited for Marissa to slip on a pair of shorts before throwing open the bedroom door. A gorgeous woman with dark skin and wavy hair stood on the other side.

"Kamilah," Heru said, sounding surprised. An unwanted spike of jealousy surged through Marissa as the beautiful woman threw her arms around Heru, hugging him tightly.

"I came as quickly as I could once I heard of your return," she told him. Pulling away, she gave his cheek a little pat. "And don't forget; it's Kim now."

"Of course," he replied, and Marissa could hear the happiness in his voice at seeing his old friend. She didn't want to be jealous. She really didn't, but the woman seemed so exotic that Marissa felt washed out in comparison. However, as she turned toward Marissa, her eyes filled with tears, and she moved in to hug her as well.

"It truly is you," Kim whispered as she wrapped her arms around her. "Thank you. She is so exquisite," Kim told Heru cheerfully, adding, "Well done."

His luminous smile filled with pride as he agreed. The giant man blocking the doorway stepped forward and to Marissa's surprise, the two men embraced. It was one of those manly one-arm-extra-hard-slap-on-the-back hugs. She was almost as blown away by the gesture as she was the by the sight of the man's eyes. They were

101

Geb's eyes, the eyes of a God.

"This is my husband, Caleb," Kim said, pulling him forward in introduction.

Marissa held her hand out for him to shake, but instead he leaned down, engulfing her in a huge bear hug. For a moment, Marissa's feet left the ground before set to right.

An adorable set of dimples appeared on his face and Marissa couldn't help but to smile in return. He looked so kind.

"Did you know that Heru died saving Kim's life?" Caleb asked, pulling Kim against his side. "I'm very happy to see he has found his way back to you. I cannot imagine my life if I had lost her that day."

"I did not know that," Marissa admitted, and Heru looked away as if he was uncomfortable with the direction the conversation was heading.

"Perhaps we should continue this discussion in the living room. I believe the two humans are still waiting for us," Heru said, changing the subject and confirming her suspicions.

The two humans in question looked up as they entered the room as a group, but Kera glanced away as Heru passed. Marissa noticed that Weave didn't question him again, and she assumed that Kera had told him everything. The fact they remained in spite of earlier events said more than words could. Snagging a chair from the kitchen table, Heru chose a spot furthest from the couple to sit. He pulled Marissa into his lap, and she easily settled back against his chest. Heru wrapped his arms around her waist, and she felt him take a deep breath.

"I'm sorry," he said, addressing the pair. "I have no excuse for my behavior."

"You have every excuse," Weave spoke up, impressing Marissa with his bravery. "Your first duty is to protect what's yours."

An uncomfortable silence fell over the room and it seemed no one knew where to begin. Thankfully, Kim broke it.

"Oh, Marissa, I forgot to mention that your parents have arrived safely. They have gone to stay with Jacques and Chloe."

"It's good they will get to visit family while here," and they gave her some time alone with Heru, she added silently.

"The wards didn't hold," Kera said, speaking up for the first time.

Marissa felt Heru nod. "I think we must accept that we are not safe anywhere."

"If magical wards won't keep him from breaching our homes, then we need a new plan. He's not going to stay away for long before making a second attempt," Weave said, adding his thoughts to the conversation.

"I had no warning," Marissa said, feeling the need to explain. "One minute, I was alone and the next, he was there. It felt like he was keeping me held in place, and I couldn't move. It was almost as if my feet were planted in quicksand and invisible hands were physically restraining my magic," Marissa admitted, giving voice to something that had been bothering her. "But when Heru arrived, it seemed as if a barrier was thrown up in front of me, and my mind functioned again."

Heru nodded before she finished speaking. "I was enraged at the time, but as my head cleared, I realized that I had felt his connection with you break as I came through the door."

Everyone in the room held the same thoughtful expression, as if the answer stared them all in the face, but they couldn't grasp hold of it.

"What makes you different?" Kim asked Heru. "I mean, there is something about you specifically that Rani fears. I think there must be a reason he felt the need to keep you so strictly under control."

"I have a theory on that one," Heru confessed, bringing all eyes in his direction. "You see, a magical contract must be carefully worded to work in your favor.

Rani's curse will hold so long as the Kamilah still lives, of that he was very specific and clever. However, what he had not been prepared for was my body's reaction to his curse. He could not control what I would become once I shifted since we now know that is controlled by our DNA make-up." A tiny smile touched his lips. "Cats are the guardian of the underworld. He didn't realize as he cursed me to this life he also gave me the key to protecting myself and others in my presence against him. By creating me, Rani also created a tool that could be used to aid in his downfall."

Heru fell silent and his body tensed. Tilting his head to the side, he seemed to go on high alert as he listened to something that only he could hear.

"It seems we are hosting a party tonight," he muttered as the door was thrown open so hard it slammed against the wall. A loud gasp rang out as a blood-soaked Dan crossed the threshold, followed closely by a stoic-looking Jazz.

Pointing at Kera and Weave, Dan barked, "You two, let's go."

"What's happened? Whose blood is that?" Kera asked as she scrambled to her feet.

"We can't wait another two days," Dan said as Heru answered, "Lena."

"Lena, what do you mean 'Lena'?" Kera cried.

"What happened to my mom?" she asked when no one seemed inclined to answer.

Unlike Kera, Marissa had not made it to her feet yet, and she didn't think she could stand if she tried. Dan's bleak look said it all. His eyes were dead as he stared at a spot past Kera's shoulder.

"We have to go," he said finally.

Marissa found her footing as Kera, helped along by Weave, trailed after Jazz outside.

Heru followed them to the door and blocked Dan's path. "Here, you'll need this," he told Dan, grabbing ahold of his forearm. An orange light glowed beneath Heru's fingers and Dan let out a hiss from between his teeth. When Heru dropped his hand, there was a black tattoo with a red lightning bolt streaking through the center where his hand had been. Marissa stifled a shocked gasp as she recognized the symbol. It matched the one that Heru had etched into his bicep. It was the mark of a warrior.

"Your group may not cross into the Hall of the Gods without this," Heru explained. "Jazz has special privileges that allow him to go unnoticed, for the most part, but you are mortal. The stars are soldiers and without an angel as your guide they will attack," he warned. "Show them the mark and they will guide you safely there."

At Dan's solemn nod, Heru stepped aside, but Dan reached out, placing a bloodstained hand on his shoulder.

"Promise me you'll have no mercy," he demanded, staring intently at Heru.

"None lives in my heart," Heru assured him and his tone left no room for doubt he spoke anything less than the truth.

Dan gave a short nod. "Good."

"We have to leave here," Marissa announced as soon as the door closed behind Dan. "We are putting everyone here in danger with our presence. My magic is weak this far from the sea, and I need to return to it."

"You can't leave," Kim cried. "The two of you will be all alone in Martinique."

Heru wrapped his arms around Marissa's waist, showing their united front. "He'll follow us," Heru said, lending his strength to Marissa's argument. "This is the right thing to do."

Kim's face fell, signaling her acceptance of their decision. "At least let me send your parents with you," she pled, but Marissa was shaking her head before she finished speaking.

"Jazz and the others will need someone to protect their physical bodies as they travel," Marissa reminded her. "My parents are the best choice. They are powerful and their souls protected."

Caleb spoke up. "Then let us go with you. It will not be easy for this demon to take out two gods."

"And a goddess," Marissa interjected.

"Or me," Kim added.

Heru glanced over at Marissa, letting her know the final decision would be hers. She chewed her lip as she mulled it over and the seed of an idea grew.

"How fast can the two of you travel?" she asked.

*****

There was no air, only a hazy light.

"Come on, sleepy head. You have to get dressed."

The female voice was so out of place that Lena went from asleep to awake in a heartbeat. Her eyes shot open, only to squeeze shut again against the bright light of the room.

"Come on," came the voice again, this time accompanied by the sound of beating wings. Lena wanted to swat the birds away as the flapping increased.

"Grrrr, would you wake up?" the voice growled.

The flapping stopped and something solid landed on her chest. Peeking one eye open, Lena spotted a tiny one-foot tall woman with shiny wings protruding from her back, sitting on her upper body.

"Ack," Lena squealed, scrambling to sit up, and pulling the blanket with her for protection. The move sent the miniature being ass over teakettle before landing in Lena's lap. Sitting up in a huff, the tiny woman crossed her arms over her chest, and blew her brown hair out of her face.

"Shit, lady, you could've cracked a wing or something," she said, sounding angry.

Lena's mind cleared and everything came rushing back to her in an instant. In a panic, her hand shot to her throat, but the skin felt smooth and unblemished beneath her fingers.

"Am I dead?" Lena asked in a horrified whisper.

Tugging at her leather bustier and denim skirt as she stood, the sprite waved away her concerns. "Nah, you ain't dead. Samuel got to you right in time, he did."

"Who's Samuel?"

"That would be me," rumbled a deep voice from the open doorway, causing Lena to jump in surprise, and sending the pixie tumbling over again.

"Bloody freaking hell, Samuel, wear a bell, would ya?" she cried as she attempted to right herself once more. Her hair stood from her head after the fall and her green eyes flashed angrily in the giant creature's direction.

"You can fly, stupid," he shot back.

The dark warrior angel and fairy made a humorous pair staring each other down, and Lena looked back and forth between them, wondering who would win. "It's almost time," the angel finally said, breaking the silence.

"Oh yeah," the pixie chirped, and in a flash of light she disappeared before reappearing as a full-grown woman on the other side of the room. Throwing wide open the doors of a huge wooden wardrobe, she pulled clothes out from inside and tossing them aside as she rejected each one. Lena stole a moment to look around. The room was opulent to say the least. The bed was huge, and she sank in almost as if on a cloud. Everything was decorated in bright rich colors and all the wood shined. She wanted to ask more questions, but she didn't know where to start.

Samuel moved into the room and threw himself down on the bed. Lena barely had time to move her feet before he squished them, and when he landed, she bounced twice from the impact. Scooting back until his wings were up against the wall, he settled in, crossing his legs at the ankle. His chest was bare and his kilt inched up a bit high so Lena attempted to keep her eyes averted.

"Thank you for saving me," she told him, still refusing to look in his direction.

Out of the corner of her eye, she saw him shrug. "My sword weighs more than you."

Although Lena wasn't sure what that had to do with anything, she didn't say more. Her eyes strayed in his direction with no plan of doing so and she tore them away again. He was very big, and he took up too much space. That's what she was telling herself since she was happily married. Giving it up as a bad job, she stared at him openly with a happy girlie sigh. He was extremely sexy. When she thought back to every Scottish historical romance she'd ever read, she realized this man, minus the wings, was exactly what she pictured the hero to look like. Luckily, he didn't seem put off in the least by her open gawking. He was smiling as if he was having the time of his life and he seemed almost like a giant puppy in his enthusiasm. She wanted to stroke behind his ears.

Must. Not. Pet. Strange. Men, she reminded herself sternly.

"I know, I'm gorgeous," he said when she still couldn't find the will to look away.

"It's unnatural," she agreed.

"No, I assure you, this is my real hair. See, feel," he added, leaning toward her. Her hand lifted of its own accord, and his smile hitched up a notch. It hit her.

"You're fucking with me," she accused.

Samuel winked and fell back against the wall. "I'm not above using my every advantage to entice a beautiful woman, and I have many," he said, drawing out the last word.

"I have no doubt," Lena agreed, tearing her eyes away.

"I didn't catch your name," Lena said to the pixie, hoping to distract herself.

"I'm Tamara, but everyone calls me Tam," she answered without turning. "Ooh," she cried, pulling out a cream-colored satin gown. "Mistress Katrina has always been the one with the best taste. This one is perfect for you."

Lena noted the neckline that plunged to the waist. "I can't wear that," she told her, not bothering to hide the blunt note in her tone.

Tam blinked owlishly at her. "Why not?" she asked as she skipped to Lena's side with the dress dangling from one finger.

"Yeah, why not?" Samuel chimed in.

Lena glanced back and forth between the two, trying to decide which one was crazier.

"Come look," Tam said, taking Lena's hand with her free one and tugging. At her insistence, Lena slipped from beneath the covers and allowed Tam to drag her to the mirror. Standing behind her, Tam draped the dress over Lena's shoulders for full effect.

"See? It brings out the color in your eyes."

Lena didn't spare a glance for the dress. Instead, her gaze remained locked on her reflection. The face staring back at her was one she had not seen in at least twenty-five years. Every fine line and wrinkle she'd earned over the years had been erased. It was true. She was immortal. Shifting her attention to Tam, she said the first thing that came to mind. "I'm going to need something that shows a bit more cleavage."

"Mhmm, I agree," Samuel said from behind her.

CHAPTER EIGHT

"I have spent many long years recording the history of our people and keeping track of my extensive understanding of potions and spells to pass this knowledge down to my sons. However, one shall die with me.

"When you have lived as long as I have, there will come a time when the thrill of life shall abandon you. That's my only excuse for what I have done. An intriguing request from a golden stranger sent a surge of challenge through my veins, and it was too much for me to resist. It became a matter of vanity I should prove myself more powerful than fate. Could a soul choose to live a different life than the one assigned to them? If so could I create an elixir that would allow them to choose?"

-Excerpt taken from The Book of the Unknown

"Stick to the plan," Heru reminded Marissa for the third time, causing her to roll her eyes as he wrapped his arms around her waist, but he could tell there was no heat behind it. After seeing Rani with her own eyes and having him trap her in place, he was sure she was in no hurry to repeat the experience.

"I know. I will not allow us to solidify until we're sure the house is secure," she repeated by rote. "Just don't let go of me." Twining her arms around his neck, she held his gaze, and their forms shimmered. In the end, they had decided that Kim and Caleb would follow them to Martinique only after they had ensured the safety of the people of Jackson Station. After all, the point in their departure was to avoid any further loss of life and the hope was that Lena's death assuaged Rani's bloodlust for one night. Even as the surrounding room disappeared, she was a solid force beneath his touch, keeping him grounded in reality. His senses were on high alert as her kitchen came into focus, but they remained half inside another realm. The Vampire inside him made an appearance as he focused on their surroundings. His fangs lengthened at the thought of losing Marissa by returning here. The flickering lights around them faded, and the floor steadied beneath his feet, but still there was no scent of danger in the air. Marissa's grip didn't loosen even as it became clear that they were under no threat of attack. Tuning into this side of himself had been a risk, one he was feeling the ramifications of with Marissa in his arms. He remembered a moment too late to keep his fangs hidden from sight, and Marissa's eyes locked on his mouth. He tried to rein his curse back under control. Expecting to be hit with a wave of fear, her lust caught him off guard.

"Are we safe?"

In his shock, he could only nod at her question.

"Will you know if he gets close?"

"Yes," he said past his rapidly drying throat.

"Good," she breathed, pulling his head down to hers before he realized her intent. He tried turning his head to save her from this side him. She was too quick, and it was too late. His desire for her outweighed everything else. It always had. Keeping hold of a single strand of sanity, Heru kept his touch light until her tongue stroked his fangs and she moaned in response. All sanity fled as he lifted her onto the counter. Her knees spread wide to accommodate his wide frame as he ground his hips against her center. Her fingernails bit into his shoulders as he nipped at her lips. Marissa drew a sharp breath, and he jerked his head away in fear. A drop of blood clung to her bottom lip and his eyes focused in on it. The drum of her heart beat in his ears, and her sweet smell filled his lungs as he tried to gain control. She made no move to wipe away the blood. It was almost as if she tried to tempt him further. Unable to see her in pain, he captured her mouth once more long enough to stroke his tongue over the tiny cut, sealing it closed. Burying his face against her throat, he locked his jaw shut as the flavor of her blood nearly caused his control to snap. Gripping the edge of the counter, he prayed for strength while she rubbed small circles along his back as if comforting a child.

"Does it hurt? To get bitten, I mean," she added when he didn't answer her right away.

Keeping his forehead pressed to her shoulder, he answered her honestly.

116

"I don't know."

Silence stretched between them, but the thirst for her blood did not subside.

"Make love to me," she whispered, causing him to lift his head and meet her eyes. He needed her to see the hunger inside him and understand what she asked.

"I'm afraid of myself right now," he admitted.

Taking his face between her hands, she slowly drew him toward her. "Make love to me," she repeated, touching her lips to his and proving her trust. Reaching between them, he unbuttoned his jeans even as he questioned his own sanity for doing so.

"You won't hurt me," she said, reassuring him. Sliding her hand over her body, Marissa's clothes disappeared behind the trail of her touch. "I'm more powerful here," she reminded him. At the sight of her delicious body bared before him like a feast, his willpower fled. Snagging her hips, he hauled her forward until she balanced on the edge of the counter.

"Don't say I didn't warn you," he growled as he buried his shaft deep inside her welcoming heat. Her walls tightened around him and he locked his knees against the pleasure that rolled down his back. The desire to taste her blood became secondary to another need growing inside him. Rotating his hips, he pulled out slightly, and she tightened further, attempting to prevent the loss, before he surged home again. Her head collapsed against the cabinet behind her as her eyes fell closed. With her hands braced against the hard surface, she met him stroke for stroke. Dipping his chin, he stared down between their joined bodies, watching as his cock disappeared inside her before reappearing again. The sight of her juices coating his skin caused his balls to draw up tight. He slowed his pace at the sensation, fighting against the orgasm that lurked close by. He wanted to watch as she found her release. Circling her clit with his thumb, she strained to meet his touch. He wanted to keep her held on the edge, but her lightning quick orgasm took him by surprise as she cried out his name. Pride surged through him as he played witness to the ecstasy etched across her features. She was so fucking beautiful that it stole his breath away and he wanted to see her do it again. However, his body had other ideas. Drawing her close, he rocked against her, giving into its demands. Her teeth sank into his shoulder, and as if that was what he'd been waiting for, his dick pulsed inside her. With him still buried to the hilt, Marissa touched her lips to his ear.

"You're not deep enough," she said against his skin. "I'm greedy," she explained. "I want all of you."

She was luring him in with her voice, tempting him to do as she bade. The palms of her hands ran down the length of his back. As her clothes had, his shirt disappeared. Locking her ankles behind him, she pressed closer until nothing but the sweat on their skin separated them. She nipped at his earlobe before licking it in apology. Every muscle in his body remained tense and his dick couldn't have gone soft if he tried. He could hear the blood rushing through her veins, but his lust for her body was greater than his thirst. In an unconscious motion, he kneaded her hips between his hands, unable to stay completely still, but incapable of moving away. He wanted to bend her over and take her hard. He wanted to hold her like this and slowly make love to her. Forever wasn't long enough for his every want.

Her wet heat constricted around his cock. "Drink from me," she ordered, freezing the air in his lungs. Slanting away, he searched her face for any lingering doubts and found none. She knew that he would never hurt her and he did too, he realized with a start. It was the one thing he should've never feared. He was physically incapable of causing her harm. Her pain was his own. Moving slowly and giving her time to back down, Heru licked a path down the column of her throat. It was enough, he decided, even if she stopped him now. What they had was enough for him. Liquid heat flooded her core, and she squirmed against him, showing her impatience.

"I love you," he whispered before sinking his fangs deep.

Light exploded behind his eyes as her blood coated

his tongue, giving him strength. It was like nothing he had ever tasted before and power surged through him. He knew that Marissa had found her release again as he drew from her vein. Her moans echoed off the walls of the kitchen as he sealed closed the wound.

With her blood flowing through his veins, joining them in a way as never before, he felt certain of a couple of things. She was in for a long night and Kim and Caleb were in for a real show if they turned up too early.

*****

Time and distance have no meaning; Dan realized the truth of that as he traveled to the Hall of the Gods. His gut told him he was far from home, but his mind only recognized how quickly they arrived.

Nothing was as he expected. The stars that appeared as twinkling lights in the distance were actually hardened men surrounded by flickering flames. Their eyes held the same flatness as the men Dan helped over the years. After witnessing too many horrendous acts, the light would leave their eyes and they no longer felt a thing.

The Hall itself was bright and luxurious. However, instead of inducing greed or longing, Dan wanted to turn his eyes away. Something inside him recognized that it all meant nothing. From one warrior to another, the stars handed them over to the angels for escort through the palace. Kera and Weave seemed in awe as they took in their surroundings, but Dan kept his eyes locked straight ahead. His only goal was Lena. Kera touched his arm, pulling his attention her way. Her smile reminded him for a moment of the little girl he raised.

"Mom is fine. I can feel her here."

At her words, the blond angel leading their troupe turned his head, glancing back over his shoulder.

"I will take you to see your wife, but the other two mortals must stay here." He pointed at a nearby sitting room that reminded Dan of the waiting room at a doctor's office.

He protested, but Kera cut him off. "It'll be okay. I can feel her, but you need to see her. You won't feel better until you do."

The angel gave him an apologetic smile. "I cannot allow a grand parade through these sacred halls."

Even though he didn't like it, Dan dipped his head, acknowledging his acceptance. Reaching over, he gave Kera a quick hug and met Weave's eyes over the top of her head. An understanding passed between the two men. They would leave here together or die here together.

As he moved away, Jazz fell into step behind him. At Dan's questioning look, Jazz eyed the angel's back with mistrust.

"I will not send you off alone with this one. He stabbed me in the back last I was here."

Without turning, the angel snorted. "I nicked you. If I'd stabbed you, we wouldn't be having this discussion."

Their jibes became background noise as the sound of Lena's laughter drifted from an open door ahead of them. He nearly shoved the slow moving creature that blocked his path to her out of his way in his desperation to reach her. Her laughter wasn't enough. He needed to see she was unharmed. His heart rate kicked up as he turned the corner. Catching his first glimpse of her, his feet froze to the floor. In his shock, he could not move a step closer. It was Lena, but it was the one he'd married many years ago, not the one he'd watched die. Even his fingertips went numb as the full impact of what he was seeing hit him. She was young, and he was not.

Shock gave way to anger at the sight of the man with his body molded against Lena's back. Murderous rage filled his mind as he eyed the hands touching his wife's shoulders. If angels could die, this one was dead.

*****

Time moved at a different pace in the heavens and Lena wasn't aware of its passage. She was impatient to have Dan back at her side, but Samuel and Tam did their best to keep her entertained.

"No, I promise," Samuel assured her. "It tastes like

fish."

Standing at the edge of the long table laden with food, Lena eyed the dish Samuel referenced with cynicism. It didn't look like any meat she recognized, and as a matter of fact, there wasn't a single dish she felt safe trying. Leaning over her shoulder, one of Samuel's wings nearly poked her eye out as he pressed against her back.

"You should try that one," he said, pointing toward a green dish across the table. It jiggled in response, but not in a gelatin sort of way.

"I think it's trying to escape," she whispered, hoping it wouldn't hear her.

She felt more than saw Samuel nod. "It does that. You have to scoop it up quick. It's pretty light on its feet."

"Feet," she repeated, feeling numb. He chuckled at her horrified tone, but a noise from the doorway caught their attention.

Lena sucked in a sharp breath at the sight of Dan. He was wearing the same clothes as he had the last time she had seen him, except they were now covered in blood. She assumed that it was her own. His expression was devoid of all emotion except for his eyes. They burned brightly as they locked on Samuel's body leaning into hers. Her stomach quivered. She had almost forgotten this jealous side of him. It had been so long since she had seen it and it made her feel desirable.

"Your man has arrived," Samuel announced unnecessarily. "He is very puny," he tacked on, causing her to smother a giggle. Dan had always towered over every other person in the room and she'd never heard him described as puny before.

"Ah, it is the Assass`i," Samuel cheered, finally stepping away from her as Jazz appeared behind Dan.

Jazz broke out into a huge grin at the enthusiastic greeting. "What's up, Big Bird?"

"HA! You think that I don't know who that is, but I do, and he is yellow. We are nothing alike," Samuel assured him.

"No giant gold rod tonight?" Jazz asked as Samuel crossed the room to his side. Throwing his arm over Jazz's shoulders, he steered him out of the room.

"It's under my kilt. Why, do you wish to stroke it?"

"You know, bird, I have a great recipe for wings," Jazz told him. Both men roared with laughter as they disappeared from sight, leaving Dan and Lena alone. Lena wanted to run and jump into Dan's arms, but he seemed uncertain.

"I wonder if anyone else has realized yet that Jazz is capable of great emotion?" she asked, attempting to put

124

him at ease, but his expression did not change, and she fidgeted beneath his stare. "I guess he has learned to hide his feelings since he wasn't meant to have them, but he loves us," she added. "It wasn't supposed to happen, but that's the way love works. It grows. Cherish gave him the ability and then there was no stopping it." She knew that she was rambling, but she couldn't seem to stop. Clamping her jaw tight, she dropped her gaze to the floor, blinking back tears. Things weren't supposed to feel this way between them. She didn't want this distance.

"You're beautiful," he said softly, bringing her eyes back to his.

Brushing her hand over her borrowed clothes, she tugged at the short dress from Tam's personal wardrobe. It had seemed like such a good idea at the time since she had the sexiest outfits, but now she felt self-conscious in the fairy's clothing.

"I guess it's one perk of immortality. I get to have my hot young body back," she said with a nervous giggle.

"I meant on the inside," he clarified and the laughter died on her lips as he moved closer. Reaching behind him, he pulled her Tarot cards out of his back pocket. He stared down at the blood-spattered deck in his hand and brushed his thumb over them.

"Would you read them for me?" he asked, handing

them over.

In the many years they'd spent together, she had done a thousand readings for him, but only once by his request. It had been their very first date. Her hands shook as she accepted the stack from him. Placing them face down on the table next to her, she flipped the top card over. Her eyes never left his as she performed the motion. He glanced down quickly before meeting her gaze once more.

"The Queen of Cups," he said, telling her what she already knew.

"Your future hasn't changed one time over the years," she told him softly. "You have always been meant for a woman who sees visions in her cup."

Reaching up, he brushed his knuckles along the line of her jaw and she tilted her head, attempting to move closer to his touch. He followed the progression of his fingers with his eyes as they trailed a path down the column of her neck.

"I failed you." His voice held such sadness as he made his confession that Lena's chest constricted. It also pissed her off a little. She could not let this continue. She realized how small they were since being here. How little she saw of the future compared to the Fates. Most of all, Lena realized there wasn't a thing she could do to change anyone's future; she could only follow the path set for her to save the people meant to be saved. That path ran parallel to Dan's and always would.

"Dan, shut the hell up," she said as she grabbed two handfuls of his shirt and towed him forward. His eyes widened in shock at her tone, but fell closed as she went up onto her toes and slanted her mouth over his. She refused to back down. She could feel the tension leave his muscles as his tongue touched hers and he pulled her closer. Wrapping her in his embrace, he stepped closer until there wasn't an inch left between them.

"Awwww," Tam cried, fluttering around their heads, and causing Lena to let out a giggle as Dan searched for the source of the sound. He looked almost horrified at sight of the pixie flying in a circle around them.

"Um, what is that?" he asked, nodding in Tam's direction.

"Not what; whom," Tam said punctuating her words with an offended sniff. However, it didn't last long as she broke into a wide grin before cheering. "Oh, I'm so happy to see that my outfit has you ravaging Lena. It gives me such hope that one day someone will delight in my feminine curves as well." Tam covered her mouth with both hands. "Did I say that out loud?" she mumbled from behind them.

"You're wearing her clothes," Dan repeated, as if trying to work that out in his head. He had always been entirely too analytical. Tam flashed and became her full-size self.

"It isn't quite so short on me, but then Lena is very tall," she explained.

The three of them stood in silence as Dan obviously tried to absorb everything, Tam smiling as if she was attending a party, and Lena trying her damnedest not to laugh her ass off at the sight of them both.

"Tam!" Samuel roared from the doorway and she jumped a foot in the air in her surprise.

"Oh yeah," Tam chirped. "It's time," she informed them.

CHAPTER NINE

"What's going to happen to me when I drink it?"

"You'll go to sleep, that's all."

His voice was comforting. The way Marissa always pictured a father should be. Nodding her head, she took the vial between her fingers, and sat down at the edge of the bed.

"What will happen to my body?" she asked, panic welling up in her chest.

Geb placed his hands lovingly upon her shoulders and held her gaze steadily. "You don't have to go through with this," he said, giving her the chance to back out. Her spine stiffened. She could do this and she had to. Heru was out there alone and this was the only way they could be together. With one last loving look at the place their love built, Goddess Marissa tipped the vial, swallowing its contents, and leaving the only life she'd ever known behind.

-Excerpt taken from The Legend of Fire and Water

Fine threads of silver lined to the entire room, making it appear as a gigantic spider's web. Although Selena had been in charge of this place since the beginning of time, she still held her breath every time she entered, in fear of disrupting a single strand.

Each individual element was infinite yet she knew

every single one by heart, and she easily found the three strands belonging to her visitors. Hooking the shimmering threads with her fingernail, she lifted them away from their current path. She held the threads of their lives in her hands as she spoke.

"Everything is foretold," she explained. "And free will is merely an illusion. It doesn't matter what choices you make because you will always continue in the direction meant for you," she said, indicating how each one branched off several times before always ending up back on its original path.

"At the beginning of time, there was a great war between the gods. There was no Greece, Egypt, or any other mortal to split worshippers between them. There was only greed and boredom tearing at the realms. This very place was almost destroyed in the battle and thus the stars were born as guardians of the sky. The strict discipline of these warriors brought swift order and saved us from ourselves until a bargain could be struck between us. After their creation, Geb appointed his son, Heru, as their lord and master since he was well respected and the most levelheaded of our people. Eros, or as you may know him, Cupid, had a bit of a devil-may-care attitude about the whole situation. In the past, he'd enjoyed the free travel between the realms, but with Heru in charge of the door, things became more difficult for him. Since Eros loved nothing better than starting trouble, he created the Pisces as a distraction."

"Pisces," Dan repeated. "You mean the astrological sign with the two fish tied together by a rope and swimming in opposite directions?"

"Exactly," Selena said. Leaning closer to her captive audience, she watched their faces as she revealed Eros' secret. "Except, the fish was actually a beautiful woman named Marissa, and that rope represented her magical ability to capture the stars." She hardened her voice in attempt to make them understand the seriousness of what she was telling them. "No other person or being has the power to do what Marissa can. Eros' aim was deadly accurate when he chose the pair to fall in love, but while he concerned himself with only his freedom, he did not see how the power of their love would change the entire world. I see the fate of all people, but I cannot control what other Gods suddenly form with their powers. Marissa and Heru's love crafted a new realm. Their desire to be together created dreams."

Watching Selena clasp his life in the palm of her hand made Dan feel very insignificant. He was right there, hanging in the balance of her whims.

However, curiosity is the mother of all emotions. Although she could snap their lives out of existence at any moment, he needed to know what she knew. Knowledge had always been Dan's downfall. He needed to know how things worked, why they were the way they were, and how he could control them. He saw things in a way that others could not, and he knew how

131

to manipulate information to create the outcome he wanted. This was no exception. Every detail Selena handed him felt like power to him. "Is that why you kept the pair apart all these years?" he asked, keeping any hint of accusation from his voice.

Selena shook her head and her eyes filled with sadness. "Each person is responsible for their actions, and every action causes a reaction," she expounded. "They created dreams, dreams needed a guardian, and the Kamilah was created for that purpose. It was Heru's responsibility to guard the keeper of dreams until she found a new protector in her husband. You see," she explained, "Heru's star was destined to fall in Egypt."

Dan was beyond fascinated by her story, it all sounded so plausible and simple when looked at from her point of view. He could not even begin imagine the intelligence that went into this much forethought and planning.

"And what of Marissa?" he asked, and a smile touched Selena's lips.

"Are you asking to know all of my secrets?"

Was he? He wondered momentarily. As a man who created new lives for people, he felt compelled to know every detail of this place. He needed to know the outcome.

"It's as if it is a game of chess where you are the

Chessmaster, and we are the pawns," he said, avoiding her question. Since he did the very same thing for a living, he was in no position to judge. It was merely an observation.

"Someone has to be," she said with a shrug.

"Yes," he agreed. "Someone does, so what about Marissa?"

Selena surprised him by laughing. "Once upon a time, Marissa gave her life for the man she loves." She took a turn, looking each of them in the eye, as if imploring them to understand the power of her words. "And today, you will sacrifice your after-life for the world you love. I handpicked the four of you and you have been working for me your entire life; you just didn't know it. If you look back on the number of lives you have saved in one lifetime, then imagine that you can do with an eternity. I hope you will not hold it against me if I find I'm unable to allow you only one life."

Lena, being Lena, had been trying to glance in every direction at once during Selena's story. He could tell that she was enjoying herself, with zero fear for their future, as if she was at an amusement park. Of course, she'd never truly feared anything and had known this day was coming long before anyone else had. Catching sight of him watching her, she reached over and took his hand. At the motion, the four of them linked fingers, presenting a united front. Dan knew in his heart each felt the same as he did. They had made a vow to protect the world from all evil, foreign, and domestic. This was their chance to do that for countless people, and even if they had been given a choice in the matter, they would have taken her offer. Lena was already immortal, and his life was with her. Seeing the world from this vantage point, Dan couldn't hold onto his bitterness, and understood Lena's gift of sight in a way he never had before. Squaring his shoulders, Dan gave Selena a sharp nod. At his cue, she stretched the three silver threads the length of the room before securing them in place on the opposite wall beside Lena's. Dan felt the years fall away, leaving him the young man he once was.

"Go with good health," Selena whispered, freeing them from the heavens.

CHAPTER TEN

The Fate, Selena, shimmered into the room, appearing at Geb's side. The two powerful entities stared down at the Goddess' lifeless form. "It will be a long road, my dear," Selena told her quietly. "I promise you I have a plan and you will have your happily-ever-after."

"Will they hate us, do you think?" Geb asked Selena.

"For a while they will," she answered him honestly. "But a love such as theirs is worth waiting for, fighting for and dying for," she added.

Linking his fingers with hers, Geb tugged Selena closer. "A sentiment I'm all too familiar with," he told her before swooping in to capture her lips with his own.

*****

Standing shoulder-to-shoulder, Marissa and Kim stared out over the horizon, watching the stars play with the waves.

Kim tilted her head as if hearing a voice that Marissa could not.

"Heru says stick to the plan," Kim said, proving her suspicions right and causing Marissa to roll her eyes while muttering an ugly word.

"He says he heard that," Kim added, making her chuckle.

The waves lapped over Marissa's bare feet, and she nearly sighed in ecstasy. She glanced over to find Kim watching her closely.

"Can you never go home again?"

Marissa shook her head at Kim's question. "This is my home now. Truly," she assured her when a sad look passed over Kim's features. "The sea is like a friend to me now," she said, trying to explain the way she felt. "Before this, it was a prison." She heard her own words and a hint of pain wormed its way into her heart, causing her to ask, "Am I wrong to feel such bitterness toward something that I love?"

"No," Kim answered with a shake of her head. "I understand. I felt that way for a long time. It is my gift that forced me into hiding almost my entire life, but it also brought Caleb to me. To me, it is simply something I was born with and I do without thought. To everyone else," she clamped her lips shut, cutting off her own words. Crossing her arms over her chest as if she could protect her heart, Kim continued. "So many lives affected all because I have a genetic mutation."

When Marissa remained silent, Kim snorted. "Sorry, that was the scientist in me talking."

Despite the depressing tone of their conversation,

Marissa felt a smile tug at the corners of her mouth. "I wonder what the scientist in you would make of me?"

While Marissa chuckled, Kim's tone was calculating as she asked, "Does that mean you'd be willing to allow me to study a sample of your blood?" Her question only made Marissa laugh harder.

Hide. You must hide, the sea whispered, sending Marissa on high alert.

"Go," she ordered, waving Kim away from her.

At her signal, and wasting no time, Caleb appeared, wrapping his arms around Kim before disappearing once more.

He comes, the wind warned. Dipping her chin, Marissa acknowledged that she heard, and she lifted her hand to her mouth. Touching her lips to her fingertips, she placed a light kiss upon them.

"Protect me," she mouthed silently against them before stooping to send the request out on the next wave. The moment her fingers touched the water, it glimmered for a moment before rolling away.

"What a lovely sight you make," a disembodied voice said as she stood. Although the speaker had no form, she could feel the hot breath upon her neck, and she knew he was close enough to kill her right then. She prayed that Heru could see Rani even if she could not, and her eyes automatically went in search of him for reassurance. Spotting the leopard in a nearby tree, she drew strength from his presence. He stared at a spot to her left, so she stepped to her right to put some distance between her and Rani while trying not to draw attention to Heru.

"Do you ever dream of being a star?" she asked, amazed by how steady her voice sounded. Rani's form shimmered to life. He seemed more curious than malicious for the moment and she took advantage of his distraction. Taking a few more steps away, she added, "Not the blockbuster-hit-at-the-movies type of star, but the flames-licking-at-your-ass kind," she clarified.

An evil smile touched his face, and it scared her more than his near proximity. "I imagine that I know a great deal about flames licking at one's ass." His deep voice sent chills down her spine and an image of the devil passed over her mind. It was the red, two-horned, and horse-hooved one of children's nightmares, but somehow she felt as if that was what hid beneath his human-like exterior. Shaking her head, she tried to expel the picture from her brain.

"You didn't answer my question," she reminded him.

He inhaled deeply and his nostrils flared at the motion. "Hmm, I find myself curious," he admitted. "What is it about you that captivated Heru?"

His question gave her hope that Kim was breaching his mind, but as he moved closer, she had to force herself not to run, especially as he reached out and ran his hand along her bare arm. Everything inside Marissa rebelled against his touch, and terrible visions of him tearing the skin from her bones forced their way into her brain. She wanted to scream in pain even though it wasn't real.

"Is it your physical beauty?" he asked, seeming to ponder the notion. "I could strip that away."

Tears blurred her vision, but she concentrated on the water at his back, and willed it to come to her aid.

"Perhaps you have other assets," he suggested and the idea he planted of him taking her by force caused bile to rise in her throat. "Yes," he hissed. "You see it, don't you?"

The water rose at his back, and even though it almost killed her to do so she met his gaze. "If you were a star, you could find out," she said, luring him in with her voice.

He nodded. "Yes, a star would know."

She struck before he could guess at her intentions and captured him with a stream of water too powerful for him to break. Heru leapt from the tree, landing in a crouch at her feet. Kim crawled from beneath the brush and kept her power focused on him. Marissa prayed that

Kim could hold the idea in his mind that was indeed a star. It was the core of her plan he maintain that belief. After all, the secret she held close to her chest was that she had been created for this very purpose. Water swirled around Rani from toe to neck, hugging him like a tight blanket, and blocking his attempts to move. His eyes glittered with malice.

"Hurry," Marissa called. "Draw a pentagram in the sand, surrounding him."

Caleb rushed to trace the lines around him as Rani hissed words in a language she could not understand. She could feel her powers weakening as he fought hard against her. The only thing keeping him from strangling the life from her with invisible hands was the barrier Heru held between them.

"Forged by the flames of hell, and upon the sands of time, you'll drink from the glass of justice, and answer for your crimes." Tiny shards of glass formed inside the cyclone surrounding Rani's body. They tore at his skin and turned the swirling water red.

Marissa's hair whipped furiously around her face, and the waves crashed to the shore as a song carried on the violent wind. Although faint at first, the melody grew louder as several voices seemed to join in. Rani froze at the sound and turned his head toward the water as if searching for its source.

"No," he screamed. His face filled with fear for the

first time. The waves transformed, taking the shape of dozens of humanlike figures. They each shimmered to life and were clear as glass with no distinguishing features. There were no faces to show remorse or for Rani to plead with. Just as he had not shown mercy to Heru, he would find none for himself.

"You," Rani growled at Marissa with one last burst of fire. The flames met an invisible barrier that surrounded her before bouncing away, leaving her untouched.

"Your sins now recorded it nature's tome, and by water your fate is set in stone," Marissa said, finishing the words to her spell and sealing Rani's fate. The water creatures fell upon him and Rani's body froze in place, transforming into a solid white statue. Floating upon the creature's backs, he was carried into the sea before sinking into its depths.

As if watching everything through a stranger's eyes, Marissa saw Heru change into his human form before turning his luminous smile her way. The happiness drained from his face, and her confusion grew as he became taller and the ground moved closer. Her mind refused to grasp the concept that her legs would no longer support her weight.

Moving at the speed of desperation, Heru caught Marissa before she hit the ground. He could not lose her again. There are things no man can survive twice. She was conscious, but her body was drained of all power.

"It's okay," she reassured him as he clutched her tighter to his chest. His knees gave out at the sound of her voice and he fell back onto his ass as he realized she would be fine. She'd used every ounce of her energy fighting Rani, but she would recover.

With her gathered in his arms, he buried his face in her hair. His throat swelled, and he blinked back tears as the future opened up before him. They were together with nothing standing in their path.

"It's okay," she repeated, and he chuckled at her effort to comfort him when she couldn't move.

Brushing her hair away from her face, Heru stared down into the eyes of the woman who'd captured his heart with only a glance so many centuries ago.

"I burn hotter for you than any star in the sky."

Her smile was faint, but he could feel it shining through her.

"My love is deeper than the sea," she whispered.

"I know," he admitted, tracing the line of her cheek with his fingertip.

"Heru," she said, drawing his attention back to her eyes. "Can this be the last bad thing that happens for a while?" she asked, causing him to throw his head back in laughter.

"Ever as you command," he answered before sealing his promise with a kiss.

The End

ABOUT THE AUTHOR

Charity Parkerson is an award winning and multi-published author with Ellora's Cave Publishing, Midnight Books, and Punk & Sissy Publications. Born with no filter from her brain to her mouth, she decided to take this odd quirk and insert it in her characters.

*2013 Readers' Favorite Award Winner

*2013 Reviewers' Choice Award Winner

*ARRA Finalist for Favorite Paranormal Romance

*Five-time winner of The Mistress of the Darkpath

*Named one of the top 10 best books by an Indie author in 2011- Paranormal Reads

Reviews

*Best Paranormal Romance of 2012- Paranormal Reads Reviews

*Quoted in the Sydney Morning Herald as an authority on Independent Publishing.

Connect with her online:

--Website: charityparkerson.com

--Facebook:

facebook.com/authorCharityParkerson

facebook.com/TheMenofSin

--Twitter: twitter.com/CharityParkerso